Yours in Amsterdam

A Novel

Reyna Starlette

Chapter One

"I'm sorry, Gemma, but we're letting you go," my boss, Michael, says with a grimace. I now understand why he's been nervously fidgeting and blabbering nonsense for the past twenty minutes since he called me to his office.

"You're firing me?" I ask, shocked to my core. I honestly didn't see this coming. I'm good at my job. I get along well with my coworkers and Michael, who is now squirming in his seat in front of me like a nervous puppy. Hell, I was even invited to his house for a Christmas party, and I had a spa day with his wife, who is wonderful, by the way.

"I'm sorry," he says again, as if 'sorry' could replace a stable paycheck and health insurance. "The company is shifting its focus and priority areas, and your expertise is no longer needed. You're a wonderful employee, and everyone here loves you. I'm sure you'll find something soon. And I'm more than happy to wholeheartedly recommend you for any position." It's not hard to hear the sincerity in his voice.

I'm one of the event coordinators in this big marketing and advertising company. I've helped plan countless corporate events, which are mind-numbingly dull if you ask me. They're lifeless events taking place in some generic venue, or even worse, in the office, where people gather in small groups, talking numbers. Despite my personal distaste for such events, I've diligently and meticulously planned every event to the client's liking, to the point that they've raved about them and brought other clients. So imagine my surprise when I hear that I'm being fired.

"How is the company shifting its focus?" I ask.

"With the recent leadership shift, the company is being totally overhauled. We're now focusing on digital marketing, brand promotion, and entertainment. Corporate events will no longer be the focus," he tells me.

Are you kidding me? I'd have loved to work on these new projects. They're more up my alley than corporate events. But when I applied for the corporate marketing and advertising coordinator job four years ago, I inadvertently pigeonholed myself, and that's apparently my expertise now. I'm now the boring corporate event planner who can't be trusted to plan the fun and vibrant entertainment parties.

I sit up and give Michael a look I intended to be brave, but I'm sure is coming off as defeated from the sympathetic tilt of his head. Michael is a great boss. I haven't had any complaints against him in the past four years I've worked here, except for the time he made a questionable joke about a coworker. But at this moment, I have every right to be mad at him for firing me despite the reason. He looks at me discerningly. I know he's waiting for me to say something, but I keep my mouth shut and stare at him blankly.

Then he continues, "You'll have your job until the end of the month, and you'll receive a generous severance package."

"Michael, with all due respect, I don't want to come to work for the rest of the month knowing that I'm fired. I'm mostly done with the projects I've been working on. I only need to come for a day or so to finalize things," I say through gritted teeth.

Michael looks at me empathetically, his brows furrowed ever so slightly. "I understand."

Then it hits me; they've been phasing me out. I haven't been given new projects in the past several weeks, and I was wondering why. I haven't had as much free time since I started working here as I did in the last few weeks.

"Wait, is this why I haven't been given new projects to work on recently?"

"Partly, yes. The other part is, as I mentioned, the priority of the company is changing, and we no longer work on the projects you specialize in." He's calmer and more relaxed now, like a weight has been lifted off his shoulders. I, on the other hand, am sinking like a weight has been dumped on me.

After I leave Michael's office, I put my succulent, notebooks, and pens in a small box and head home with a frown on my face like the disgruntled employee that I am. I'll be back tomorrow to finalize my departure and gather my stuff, but I still want to have the full dramatic effect of a sad employee who has just been sacked. My effort is not in vain. I garner a few sympathetic looks while I walk home. For New York City, this is a massive win.

I devise a plan of action for the night. I'll order an obscene amount of food and open a bottle of wine while I wait for Justin to come home. Justin—my wonderful fiancé. At least I have him. Justin and I have been dating for four years. We've been living together in our apartment, well, his apartment, to be exact, on 46th Street for the past three years. He proposed six months ago. Naturally, I said "yes" before he even finished asking the question. Who would say 'no' to Justin? He's the greatest.

Weighed down by the horrible news I just received and the thirty-minute walk it's taken me to get here, I stumble into the elevator. I can't wait to collapse onto the couch in my apartment.

When I open the front door, I hear a noise coming from the bedroom. The noise grows louder as I walk into the living room. It sounds like a donkey on labor if I didn't know better.

Oh no, this is not happening. I fling the bedroom door open, only to be stopped in my tracks by the shocking scene playing out in front of me. Justin is pounding some slender brunette from behind.

They are startled mid-stroke by the noise of the door being flung open and by my loud gasp. Justin retracts his penis from whichever hole it is in and sits on the bed facing me. The brunette scrambles to cover her body with sheets. When she turns around with a sheet covering her chest, I recognize her.

"Mindy!" I exclaim. The brunette is none other than Mindy, Justin's long-time friend. Also, my friend, at least I thought so.

Chapter Two

I stand frozen by the door, still shocked by the scene I just stumbled upon. I don't know how long I stand there. Is this really happening? I strain my eyes, hoping it's just a figment of my imagination. I'm questioning my reality. I feel like my brain is glitching. My Justin wouldn't do anything like this, would he?

But the proof is right in front of me. Justin and Mindy are right in front of me, covering their naked bodies with a sheet. Justin is looking at me with an expression I can't quite discern. Is it embarrassment? Fear? Or concern? Mindy is not even meeting my gaze; she's staring at the duvet pushed to the foot of the bed. My duvet.

They've always said they are platonic friends whenever someone questioned their friendship. They even swore that they considered each other like brother and sister. And I fully believed that, to the point that I wouldn't question them if I found them sleeping in the same bed with clothes on. But even as an only child, I know you don't do that with a brother or a sister. These little fucks.

I finally fully register what I'm seeing, and I'm pissed.

"Are you kidding me, you little shits?" I hiss, looking around for something heavy to throw their way.

"Wait, Gem. I can explain," he blabbers.

I drag a chair, making a squeaky noise that I hope will annoy the hell out of them, and sit in front of them. "Well, explain then," I say casually, like a person getting ready for a business negotiation.

I know he didn't expect me to let him explain. He was counting on me storming out. He must have forgotten that I don't back down from confrontation.

"Ah...I...mean," he stutters.

Mindy is mute. She's just sitting there, gawking at me with her big eyes, when she finally has the courage to look at me. I trusted her like I trusted Justin. I even confided in her when Justin and I had fights, and she gave me advice. Have I been a complete idiot?

"You said you can explain. Fucking explain, then." I wait for his response with resolve.

"It was a mistake," he mutters.

I cackle loudly, but there is no joy in my voice. "You accidentally fell into Mindy's vagina? If that's where you were. 'Your best friend, your sister'!" I say with air quotes.

He doesn't respond.

I turn to Mindy. "And you, do you have anything to say to me?"

"I'm sorry, Gem," she responds with a voice barely louder than a whisper.

"You're sorry for what? For sleeping with my fiancé on my own bed or for getting caught?" I ask, my voice bitter and dry.

"It was never my intention to hurt you," her voice breaks a little.

I see her eyes are glistening with tears, and there's a light tremble to her hand when she raises it to tuck her hair behind her ear. Then, I look at Justin. The color is drained from his face. He looks like a days-long cadaver.

There is no point in continuing this conversation. No amount of explanation or shaking in their boots can make what they did okay. The more I hear them talk, the angrier I become. I don't want to look at their cheating faces for one second longer.

"Now, get your cheating asses the hell out of my apartment. Both of you," I yell, getting up and pointing my finger to the door.

"But this is my apartment," he utters quietly. The audacity.

Mindy is already gathering her clothes and throwing them on.

"Don't you dare start with me, Justin," I hiss. My face must have been scary because he quickly puts on his clothes and heads to the door.

I wait for them, holding the apartment door open. Mindy scurries out like she's afraid I'm gonna kick her ass.

Justin looks at me and opens his mouth before he leaves. But I slam the door in his face without giving him a chance to speak.

As soon as they leave, I throw myself on the couch, deflated. How the hell did I lose two of the most important things in my life in just less than two hours? Justin and I have been together for almost four years. That is how long I've had my job. Everything I've worked for in the past four years crumbled in front of my eyes.

I don't exactly know how to feel. I know I'm hurt. But my emotion is far from sadness. Instead, it's closer to anger. I can feel every fiber in my body sizzling with fury. I'm feeling an all-consuming rage — a rage that is threatening to spill out of me. I need an outlet. No amount of fantasizing about what I'd do to Justin and Mindy is enough. And I have a pretty vivid imagination.

I put on my running gear and head out of the house. Before I know it, I'm fully sprinting without a warm-up, dodging rushing New Yorkers left and right. I run until my legs nearly give out. I run until I almost pass out. I run from my problems. I run until my heartbeat is off the chart, not giving my heart an opportunity to break.

***

It's several hours later. I'm sitting in my apartment, staring into the abyss. The TV is blaring, but I'm not paying attention. I still haven't fully processed the shit show my day has turned out to be. I don't know what my next move is. The only thing I certainly know is that I have to move out. This is Justin's apartment, and the lease is in his name.

He made that clear when he texted me earlier: *I'm spending the night at Jeremy's. I'll come home tomorrow. I can't stay out of my apartment for long. I know you're hurt. But we can work this out.*

He said, "I know you're hurt," as if he's not the one who hurt me, as if he didn't throw away what we've built over the past four years. To be honest, I'm more angry than hurt.

With no job, no place to live, and no viable prospects, I don't see a reason to stay in New York. I'll burn through my savings in just a few months if I remain here. I consider leaving town for a while, but where would I go?

I'm a New Yorker, born and raised. This is the only place I've called home my entire life. The only times I've lived outside of this city were during a year in London as a grad student and a few summers with my uncle's family in Michigan while growing up. It's tough to survive in New York without a job, unless you have substantial savings or family support to fall back on.

My only option is to stay with my mom in her one-bedroom apartment on the Lower East Side. She would take me in, no questions asked, and I could stay with her until I find something. My mom's place has always been a home waiting for me with an open door. But at this moment, I can't help feeling like a big failure. I've worked so hard to end up jobless and living with my mom at this age.

At twenty-eight, I thought I had my life figured out, until the rug was pulled right from underneath me just moments ago. Now, I feel lost.

Just as I start drowning in self-pity, my phone rings. It's Sophie, my friend from the Netherlands.

"Hey, Sophie," I answer the phone with a groggy voice, looking at Sophie's gorgeous face on my phone screen.

Her big smile fades into a frown at the sight of my face. "What's wrong?" she asks. Of course she knows something's wrong before I even say anything.

I sigh deeply and recount the day's events in detail. Sophie's face goes through every emotion as I retell the story of how, in less than twenty-four hours, I ended up jobless, single, and potentially homeless—well, I know I won't be homeless as long as my mom is here, but this is the closest I've ever gotten to homelessness. She gasps, grits her teeth in anger, and rolls her eyes through it all.

"I'm so sorry, babe. That's awful," she says with her accent, a mix of posh British and Dutch native.

"I know. I'm now jobless, homeless, and fiancéless," I say, fully embracing self-pity.

"What the fuck is wrong with Justin?" Sophie exclaims, her nose flaring in anger. "Honestly, I sometimes wonder why we even bother with men."

I release a snort at her reaction. "We bother in the hopes of finding rare gems like Lucas," I say, referring to Sophie's fiancé.

Her face lights up at the mention of Lucas's name. "I know, he's a sweetheart. I don't know what I did in my past life to deserve that man," she swoons.

Even in my heartbroken state, it makes me happy to see Sophie blissfully in love.

"But who knows at this point? We thought Justin was all that too. I'm gonna remind Lucas all the horrible things I'd do to him if he ever cheats on me, just in case," she adds.

"Stop harassing that poor man," I laugh.

"So what are you thinking?" she asks somberly.

I know what she's asking, even if she doesn't spell it out. She's asking what my plan is about my work and living situation. The problem is, I don't know. For the first time in a long time, I'm at a complete loss. I had a well-thought-out and carefully-crafted plan for the next several years of my life before everything fell apart.

"I don't know," I say softly, my voice sounding defeated even to myself. "I'll stay at my mom's place until I figure things out."

After a moment, Sophie's expressive face brightens as if a light bulb went off in her head.

"I have an idea. Why don't you come to Amsterdam and stay until the wedding?" she says, prematurely excited.

I shoot her a confused look, tilting my head to the side and raising my eyebrow. "But the wedding is a month away. What will I do there until then?"

Sophie is getting married in a month, and I'm part of her wedding party. I'm supposed to fly to the Netherlands a few days before the wedding.

"You can help me with wedding planning; it'll take your mind off things. It's perfect. My wedding planner just quit on me. And you know how bad I am at planning and organizing stuff," Sophie pleads with a hopeful voice.

"Wait, why did your planner quit?" I ask, surprised. I thought the wedding planning was on track. As an event planner myself, the idea of Sophie being without a planner a month before her wedding gives me anxiety.

"She had a family emergency. It's a long story," she responds with a nonchalant tone.

"Oh my God, Soph. How are you not freaking out? The wedding is only a month away," I say, freaking out on her behalf. A month isn't nearly enough time to find a good wedding planner willing to take over an event another planner has started.

"What's the worst that could happen? It's just a wedding," she brushes off my urgency. "But the most important thing is, now you can be my planner. It works out perfectly," she adds, returning to her excitement.

"I don't know," I hesitate, knowing I should probably focus on finding a new job and a place to live rather than traveling abroad. Going to Amsterdam sounds amazing right now, but my problems won't magically disappear when I return.

Sophie leans toward the screen, batting her eyes. "Come on, it'll be your own little Eat, Pray, Love journey."

"Where do I even stay for a month?" I ask, my voice giving away the fact that I'm actually entertaining the idea. Sophie isn't one to bother with logistics. She's as spontaneous as they come.

"Remember I told you Lucas and I just moved to our new house? My apartment in Amsterdam is empty, and we still have the lease for the next month," she responds.

"Oh wow, that's tempting," I admit. It's a pretty sweet deal to stay in Amsterdam for a month with no rent. But I don't know if running away from my problems is the right thing to do. I need to put my life back together.

"I'm telling you. It's fate," Sophie exclaims.

"Okay, I'll think about it."

Sophie and I met in London during grad school at University College London. We clicked the moment we met at orientation and decided to rent a flat together. Even after we moved back to our respective home countries, we kept in touch. The distance didn't dim our friendship. We talk several times a week, take vacations together every year, and Sophie often visits me in New York. Her family is loaded, and she works in the family business, so money has never been a problem for her. She takes spontaneous weekend trips to New York whenever she's bored, which makes the distance between us not feel as long.

After I hang up the phone, I contemplate Sophie's offer. I'm not a spontaneous person who takes random trips without meticulously planning way in advance. But when everything I meticulously planned falls apart, I can't help but wonder if spontaneity is the answer.

Chapter Three

Surprisingly, I sleep very well for someone whose life is turned upside down without a warning. I sleep as if I have no worries in the world. But when I wake up in the morning, I start crying before I even open my eyes. My anger has subsided, and the pain is taking over. I can't remember the last time I was this sad and heartbroken. How is this happening to me? I don't even know what I'm sad about the most. Losing my job? Being cheated on by the person I loved and trusted the most? Or not knowing what my next move is? I just feel so lost.

I drag myself out of bed and go to the bathroom, tears streaming down my face. I look at my reflection in the mirror. My eyes are red and clouded with tears, bags forming underneath. My curly hair is all over the place, partly covering my swollen face. I gather my hair in a bun and splash cold water on my face. I can't even bring myself to wash my face properly.

As I look up, I have clarity on what I need to do. I've meticulously planned my life and lived without straying from the plan my whole life. Look where that got me. It's time to go rogue. It's time to be spontaneous and take chances.

The opportunity has clearly presented itself last night. As Sophie said, it's fate, even if I'm not sure if I believe in that. It's decided.

I open my laptop and book a flight to Amsterdam for the next day. I'm not even going to give myself time to get cold feet. I've never made this sort of rushed decision before. To be honest, it's exhilarating.

Today will be my last day at work and in this apartment. I'm going to Amsterdam.

It doesn't take me long to finalize what I need to take care of at work. I close the projects I can close and delegate tasks that need a longer time to complete. I say my goodbyes to my coworkers, most of whom are pleasant people. Many of them seem to be surprised by my departure, which is a little consolation. It's like everyone agrees that I'm a good employee and don't deserve this.

I also find out that I'm not the only one who was let go. A handful of people from different departments have also been fired due to the new changes the company is implementing. It doesn't make me feel good by any means, but it at least finally makes me realize that the reason why I lost my job has nothing to do with me. There's nothing I could've done to prevent it. It's not me; it's the company.

I'm getting more excited about my trip as I pack in the evening. I've been to Amsterdam a few times when I was living in London, but not for more than a couple of days at a time. This time, I get to fully immerse myself in the charm of this beautiful city and Dutch culture. If I'm going to go on a spontaneous trip across the Atlantic, I intend to take full advantage of everything the city has to offer.

Justin is coming home tonight, and we'll have our last talk. I want to close that door fully before my trip in case there is lingering hope from his side that we'll come back from this. We won't.

When he comes home around eight, I'm ready. I'm calm and less angry. I sit by the dining table, sipping my tea. The moment I see him open the door and walk inside, I get a flashback of what I saw yesterday. It's like the memory of him in bed with Mindy has replaced all the memories we've made over the last four years. That's the only thing I see when I look at him now.

He walks toward me sheepishly. I don't know if his look is embarrassment or fear of what's to come. After all, he knows I'm not one to back down from confrontation. If only he knew that I've reached the point of not caring to even fight.

He sits opposite me, looking everywhere but at me. We don't exchange greetings or niceties. I just sit there and wait for him to speak first.

He finally looks up at me. "First of all, I want to tell you how sorry I am. You don't deserve this." His speech comes off as rehearsed. I wonder if he's planned and practiced what he wants to say before coming here. But that doesn't sound like Justin. He is a wing-it-and-see-what-happens kind of guy.

"I know, I don't," I say shortly.

"I know you're hurt. I totally understand if you hate me. But I want to work this out. I don't think we should throw

18

away what we've built for this. I'll give you time if you need time. I'll do anything to win your trust back," he says, looking deeply into my eyes with his deep brown eyes.

But those eyes don't have the same effect on me anymore. All I see in his eyes now is how he cheated on me with our mutual friend. How he looked me in the eyes several times and told me that Mindy was like his sister.

"Justin, it's over. There is no coming back from this," I say, sliding the engagement ring on the table.

His gaze follows the ring until it's right in front of him. Then he looks up. His eyes are tear-streaked.

"I love you, Gem. I don't wanna lose you," he whispers.

"You should've thought about that before you fucked 'our friend' on the bed we shared," I say, putting air quotes around the term 'our friend.' I didn't expect this level of betrayal from Justin. He hasn't given me any reason to doubt him. Maybe I've been totally blinded by his charm and the love I have for him. Were there red flags that I've missed?

He says nothing. He just looks down. I have a feeling that it was not a one-time thing. They wouldn't have the audacity to fuck on my bed for the first time.

"How long have you been sleeping together?" I ask. He's known Mindy for more than ten years. So, who knows? They might have been each other's sidepieces the whole time.

"We've done it a few times over the years. But you have to believe me, Gem. It's nothing serious," he pleads.

I don't hear the last thing he says. All I think about is Justin and Mindy sneaking around behind my back for years. Now, I can't look at all the times they were alone or the times we took trips as a group in the same way.

"It doesn't matter. I'm moving out tonight," I tell him.

"You know you don't have to, right? I can stay in the spare bedroom." He stretches his hands to touch mine resting on the table. I retract my hands before he reaches them.

"I don't want to live under the same roof with you anymore," I say firmly.

"Where are you gonna go?"

"That's none of your business," I say. I'm staying in a hotel for the night, and I'll be flying to Amsterdam the next day. But he doesn't have to know that. He lost that privilege when he did what he did.

He stays quiet for a moment, and I don't speak either. The silence is deafening.

"Why were you home early?" he asks, breaking the silence.

I almost open my mouth to tell him about losing my job. I used to tell him everything. He's been my closest confidant for so long that I almost forget he can't be that anymore. He doesn't deserve to know what's going on in my life. He doesn't deserve to know about my job, or lack thereof, and my trip to Amsterdam.

"I don't need a reason to come to the place I call home whenever I want," I say. There's nothing more to say. And just like that, it's over.

I drag my large suitcases and say, "Goodbye, Justin" before I walk out. Then, I leave.

Chapter Four

If you had told me two days ago that I'd lose my job, my fiancé, and my apartment, and would be heading to Amsterdam in less than forty-eight hours, I'd have laughed in your face. Saying, 'I didn't see this coming,' is an understatement. But here I am at JFK boarding a plane, and I'll be at Schiphol Airport in just seven hours.

I keep myself occupied as I wait for my flight, alternating between watching a movie and reading a book. If I'm doing something, I won't drown in self-pity or overthink my life choices. My strategy proves to be effective. I barely think about Justin or my job when I'm lost in the story of the book I'm reading or the movie I'm watching.

My flight is uneventful for the most part, except for the guy sitting in the middle seat constantly poking my ribs. He's not doing it intentionally or maliciously. He's just too tall for the ever-so-tiny economy seats. His limbs spill over every side of the seat, and his legs protrude into the seat in front of us. He looks so uncomfortable that I feel bad for him, even if the constant poking is annoying. To make matters worse, he looks at me apologetically every time he invades my space. So I have to do that little dance of tilting my head and smiling tightly to let him know that it's fine. The whole situation is awkward and uncomfortable. So I feel over the moon when we finally land.

Sophie picks me up at Schiphol Airport with her sleek Mercedes. She jumps up and down, her hair bouncing, when she sees me coming out of the terminal. Wearing a light trench coat with a mini skirt and boots, she looks as glamorous as ever. Her blonde hair is cut short in an asymmetrical bob that frames her slim face, her sharp jawlines giving her a chiseled look.

"Sophie!" I screech, attempting to run to her while pushing my trolley. I almost knock down a family of four trying to walk across.

Sophie engulfs me in a hug, wrapping her long arms around me. Sophie is tall, while I'm five-four on a good day. I'm considered short in the US, or maybe even average, but in the Netherlands, I'm a minion.

After saying our 'how are you's' in between hugs, we load my luggage in the trunk, both of us grunting at how heavy my suitcases are. I pretty much packed all my life's worth in these suitcases.

We settle on the highway after sifting through the airport traffic.

"I'm so glad to have you here, although I don't love the circumstances that brought you," Sophie says, briefly glancing at me.

"I know, my life sucks. But at least I'm not stranded in New York with no job and apartment or sleeping on my mom's couch," I say with a faint smile. I'm really trying to find the silver lining here.

"Look at the bright side; you've been saying you're not happy with your job for the past year. This gives you an opportunity to think about your next career move."

Sophie is a glass-half-full kind of person. So, it doesn't surprise me that she found a silver lining in all of this. But then again, she's never had to worry about money her whole life, and she can afford to take as much time as she wants to think about her next career move. Me? Not so much. My savings can't even last me for six months without an income.

But she's not wrong about me not being happy with my job. My corporate events planning job paid the bills, but my real passion is starting my own event planning business. Not just any event, but I want to plan events for special day celebrations. I want to plan events that people fondly think about for years. I want to create memories. I just haven't had the resources to quit my job and pursue that full-time.

"You're right," I say.

"And fuck Justin," she exclaims, her eyes fixated on the road stretching in front of us. "You're way too good for him anyway. I don't even know what you saw in him. He has the personality of a wet towel."

I laugh. Sophie is the ultimate hype woman. She would tell me I'm better than Beyonce without missing a beat if I needed to hear that. Although we all know that's virtually impossible. No one can be better than Beyonce.

When we enter the city center, Amsterdam is as bustling as ever, crowded with tourists and locals. It's early

March, and the weather is still on the colder side. But everyone seems to be out and about, Dutch locals biking with impressive efficiency and tourists trying to keep up. You can tell who is local and who is a tourist by the way they bike, especially in the city center.

Amsterdam has more bikes than people. The biking culture is deeply ingrained in society, and the city is built around that culture. Almost every part of the city has a bike lane, as biking is the primary mode of transport for most residents. Even after having been to Amsterdam a few times, I'm still not used to seeing so many bikes in one place. I always wonder how people can locate their bikes in the sea of bikes in some of the largest parking spaces in the city. They all look the same too. If I lived here, I'd have an obnoxiously colorful and custom-embroidered bike that I could see from a mile away. That's the only way I'd be able to keep track of it.

Sophie's apartment is only a five-minute drive from Amsterdam Centraal station. It's in an old building that has been recently renovated, as Sophie tells me. The apartment is on the top floor of a four-story building that overlooks one of the beautiful canals of Amsterdam. It's a spacious space, at least by Amsterdam and New York standards, with two bedrooms and a balcony on the canal side.

The view from the balcony is a perfect window into what this city offers and its culture. I have a clear view of the canal, the narrow streets, and the buildings that characterize the unique architecture of Amsterdam. Tourists would kill to stay in this place. I can't believe I get to live here for a month.

Sophie shows me around the apartment, explaining everything I need to know. "I've stocked the fridge with all of your favorites. If you need anything, there's an Albert Heijn two blocks down," she says, opening the fridge. I remember from my previous visits that Albert Heijn is one of the supermarket chains in the Netherlands.

Glancing inside, I notice that the fridge is filled to the brim. It could easily feed a family of five for a week. She then takes me to the bike garage to show me where her bike is parked. She has left her spare bike for me. I'm overcome with emotion by her thoughtfulness.

After the tour, we settle on the couch in the living room, sipping the green tea that Sophie just made.

"You know how bad I am at planning. There's still so much to be done before the wedding, and I'm beginning to feel stressed. Lucas is away for work most of the time, so he can't be much of a help," Sophie tells me.

"Don't worry. I love planning and organizing. I'm at your service for the next month," I reassure her.

Sophie's smile widens. "Great. I'll prepare a list of everything that needs to be done. By the way, you have to come for Sunday dinner at my parents' place in Zandvoort. We'll discuss the wedding plan then. But now, I have to run. I have a meeting in thirty minutes," she says, getting up and grabbing her purse and keys.

"Thank you, Soph. I don't know what I'd do without you." I hug her tightly to show my appreciation. I'm deeply grateful to her. She's always been there for me whenever I needed her, even at times when I didn't realize I needed her.

"I should be the one thanking you; you're my maid of honor slash wedding planner now," she says, heading to the door. "Call me or text me if you need anything," she calls out as she leaves.

I step onto the balcony, looking down at people walking around and biking. Some are sitting by the canal. On the other side, there's a bar with a terrace right next to the canal. The place is packed for an early Friday afternoon. Despite the chilly weather, several people sit on the terrace, enjoying beers. It looks like they're having an early start to the weekend.

I take a deep breath, taking it all in. This is exactly where I'm supposed to be. Who gets to live in an apartment right in the center of Amsterdam without paying rent? I can find a silver lining in the mess my life has turned out to be.

Chapter Five

The following day, I decide to bike around the city. After all, it's the best way to explore Amsterdam, or any Dutch city for that matter. I'm not an experienced biker by any means. Even as a child, I didn't ride a bike often, not only because I grew up in New York City but also because my mom couldn't afford to buy me my own bike. I learned how to bike during my summer stay at my uncle's in Michigan. It's been years since I last rode a bike. But they say, 'You never forget how to ride a bike.' So, I'm putting all my trust in my muscle memory to get me through my biking adventure today.

I leave my apartment around eight in the morning, hoping the biking traffic will be lighter. But as I quickly realize, Amsterdam city center never sleeps. There are still many bikers, too many for my taste, crowding the bike lane. It also appears that I'm the only slow biker. I guess the slow tourists have understandably decided to sleep in on Saturday morning. With my nervous and slow biking, I stick out like a sore thumb. I can tell some of the other bikers are annoyed with me.

I only bike for less than a mile before I realize that this is a bad idea. I should've brushed up on my biking skills in less crowded areas before throwing myself into the lion's den. After enduring some frustrated glances and grunts from the other bikers, I decide to make a right turn, hoping to get away from the city center. But my failure to give a hand gesture to signal a turn, coupled with my slow turn, has almost made the woman behind me slam right into me. But she maneuvers with impressive efficiency and passes me on the left, yelling something at me in Dutch.

Feeling flustered, I swerve to the right in a fateful attempt to give her enough space. A space she doesn't even need anymore. She's long gone, pedaling with the speed of light. Before I know it, I hit the curb and fly off my bike, landing hard on the pavement.

While I'm trying to register what just happened and where I hurt myself, I see a silhouette towering over me. I look up at the tall silhouette, shielding me from the morning sun. It's a man in running gear.

"Gaat het?" the man says, crouching down to me. I look at him blankly. Looking at my confused expression, he says, "Are you okay?"

"I don't know," I say honestly. My knee hurts, but I don't know how badly I hurt myself.

"Let me help you up," he says, stretching out his hand. I take his hand without saying a word. Wrapping one arm around my upper back, he lifts me up with ease.

"Ouch," I exclaim as I land on my feet. My left knee hurts so much. When I look down, I realize that it's bleeding profusely.

"Does it hurt? Are you able to walk?" he asks. His voice is deep, with an accent that's a mix of an American and native Dutch speaker.

Even in my physically hurt and bruised ego state, I still recognize how sexy his voice is. He's also very tall, even by Dutch standards. He towers over me even when I'm standing.

"It does. But I can walk," I say, stepping in place to demonstrate.

He is still supporting me with his arm even though I don't physically need the support anymore. "You need a bandage for your knee."

"I know," I say, looking down at my knee exposed by my mini dress again, which is not at all weather-appropriate, by the way. I realized that the moment I stepped out of my door earlier. I just didn't have the will to go back up and change.

"I live here." He points at the building next to where we are standing and adds, pointing down at my knee, "I can help you with that."

I hesitate. I don't know this man. I certainly know it's not a good idea to follow him to his apartment. I look at my knee again. My blood is running down, almost reaching my beloved white Air Force shoes. Hell no!

"Okay. But you better not be a serial killer or something," I mutter, as though saying it out loud would make it unlikely.

"I'm not," he says. Then, he adds under his breath, "Then again, that's exactly what a serial killer would say."

I jerk my head to him with concern. Instead of a devilish grin, as I expected, I see the most captivating smile plastered on his face. I stare for longer than the situation calls for and smile back, almost against my will.

"Let's park your bike first, and then we can head up." He grabs my bike from where it's lying, locking it in the parking spot in front of his building. I watch him in silence. Apparently, chatty Gemma has left the chat.

"Come on," he says, walking to his building. "Do you need help?" he asks when we reach the front steps.

"I'm okay."

He lives on the third floor, or second floor by European counting. I cautiously climb the stairs behind him, trying to make sure not to put too much strain on my knee.

When we enter his apartment, he gestures for me to sit on the huge gray sofa and disappears into a room that I assume is the bathroom. I make sure not to spill my blood all over his couch when I sit down. I look around the spacious living room decorated in subtle colors. There's a larger-than-life flat-screen TV propped in front of the couch I'm sitting on. A couple of comfortable-looking armchairs are lined on each side of the couch. I see medical journals on the coffee table, which makes me wonder if the good Samaritan works in the medical field.

I bet some of the books on the giant bookshelf taking up the right side of the wall are medical books too. I cock my head to the left to look at the kitchen and the dining area. This massive space in the center of Amsterdam must have cost a fortune.

I hear the door open, and the good Samaritan walks toward me, holding a first aid kit. He sits next to me on the couch and asks, "Do you mind?" before touching my injured leg.

I shake my head. Then he grabs my leg and props it on his lap. I audibly gasp, but he doesn't notice. I honestly didn't expect that. I thought he was asking if I minded him touching my leg. But I realize, to my utter surprise, that I don't mind this either, not one bit. My knee hurts less in this position, and his legs feel warm against the back of my ankle.

He cleans my wound with gauze pads and some kind of solution. I grimace when the pad rubs against my open wound. I must have tensed against his lap because he looks up and asks, "Does it hurt?"

"A little. But I'm fine."

I have a chance to take a good look at him—more like gawk at him, as someone studying an abstract painting—while he was working on my knee, which makes me appreciate how handsome he is. His shortly cut dark blonde hair falls on his forehead as he looks down at my leg resting on his lap. His light five o'clock shadow gives his otherwise clean features a rugged look, emphasizing his sharp jawlines. His running t-shirt exposes his tall and lean body. I stare, mesmerized, as his muscles flex when he's carefully rubbing what I assume is an antibiotic cream on my knee. He's too focused on his first aid duties to notice me gawking at him.

When he looks up at me, I notice his deep blue eyes. His picture is probably next to the definition of 'piercing blue eyes' in the dictionary. And he looks strangely familiar, though I can't place him anywhere.

He bandages my knee and announces, "All done."

"Thank you so much," I say, carefully removing my leg from his lap and placing it on the floor.

"Are you a medical doctor or something?" I then ask.

"No," he laughs. "I only cleaned your wound and bandaged it. That doesn't require a medical degree."

"I know that. I asked because of the medical journals on the coffee table," I say, smiling. I can't help it; his smile is contagious.

"Oh, that. I'm a biomedical engineer. Plus, I have a personal interest in medicine."

"Cool," I nod. I don't know what else to say. His gaze is making me nervous for some reason, but I don't break eye contact. I stare into his deep blue eyes until he averts his gaze. I wonder how he looks extremely confident and a little shy at the same time.

"I'm Daan, by the way," he says.

I realize that I followed this man to his apartment without even asking his name. Not that it would make a difference or protect me in any way if he turns out to be a deranged serial killer or something.

"I'm Gemma," I say.

"Oh, Gemma, that's a beautiful name," he says. My name has never sounded sexier.

"Thanks. Don't tell my mom that, though. She'll go on this long rant about how she came up with the name and how it perfectly fits me," I grin. What a weird thing to say to a person I just met? I realize that as the words leave my mouth. He doesn't even know my mom or that I have a mom. I don't know why I'm feeling flustered.

To his credit, he laughs at my sad attempt at a joke. "I'm sure that's an interesting story."

"Not when you hear it as a bedtime story as a child and every year on your birthday since then," I tell him.

"Do I get to hear the story, or should I wait until I get a chance to ask your mom?"

"It's not as interesting as you might think, or as my mom presents it to be. It came from a book my mom was obsessed with when she was pregnant with me. Apparently, the story of a queen trying to find a precious stone that can save her kingdom resonated with her so much that she decided to name her first and only child after the precious stone, not even the queen," I tell him, rolling my eyes, but my face beaming with the thought of my mom.

His deep, growling laugh reverberates through the room, which has a weird effect on the way my heart beats.

"I take it you're American? So what brought you to Amsterdam?" he asks.

It takes everything in me not to blurt out, 'I was fired from my job, and I caught my fiancé cheating.' But I decide against trauma dumping on this handsome stranger.

"I needed a break from New York, and I have a friend here," I say curtly. By 'New York,' I mean my crumbling life there, not the city. I'd never get tired of the city. It's the greatest city in the world, and no one can change my mind. That's a hill I'm willing to die on.

"I get that. Who doesn't need a break from New York?" he says.

I narrow my eyes and glare at him suspiciously, eyebrows furrowed and head tilted. Does this man just insult New York? I don't know which is worse: this blunder or turning out to be a deranged creep.

"You don't like New York?" I ask, my tone suggesting that his answer could change everything.

"Not really. It's nice to visit and spend a few days in. But to live? No. It's not for me," he responds without noticing the not-so-subtle change on my face.

Here I was thinking how perfect-looking this man is, and then I find out that he doesn't like New York. I don't know if his dashing good looks can make up for this major character flaw. Yes, I said it; not liking New York is a character flaw.

"What? New York is the greatest. Why wouldn't you like to live there?" I raise my hands in disbelief. I'm flabbergasted.

"It's loud, crowded, not very clean… should I keep going?" he smirks.

"It's also the center of art, fashion, and culture," I retort.

"I beg to differ on that," he says, flashing an amused smile. Apparently, he finds me getting riled up amusing.

"The United Nations headquarters is located in New York," I pull out my last card. Surely, that should be convincing.

"You're right. The international rat convention also happens there," he chuckles. I look at him incredulously, but his deep, growling laugh is so contagious that I can't help but laugh too.

"Have you lived in New York?" I ask, not letting go of his contempt for my city.

"No, but I used to go there often when I was living in Cambridge."

Aha! This is my gotcha moment. "Why did you go often if you don't like it?" I say triumphantly.

He shakes his head, as if the idea of me taking issue with him not being fond of New York is crazy. "As I said, it's a nice city to visit. There's so much to do and see. But you can't pay me to live there."

I give up. He's not changing his mind about New York City. Instead of harping on that, I ask, "What were you doing in Cambridge?"

"I went to MIT for undergrad and also worked there as a researcher after I graduated."

"If you like living in Cambridge, I'm not surprised that you hate New York," I say, apparently unable to resist harping.

"What's wrong with Cambridge?" he asks, throwing his hands up in an exaggerated display of disbelief. He's imitating my earlier reaction.

I stifle a laugh, biting my lips.

"Nothing, except being a complete snoozefest," I say, faking a yawn to drive my point home.

He laughs. "Touché. But how do you like Amsterdam?"

"I love Amsterdam," I exclaim.

"Finally, a city we can agree on," he responds, sounding very excited.

"Yay," I say and hold my hand up for a high five. I don't know why I did that. Am I twelve? But there is no going back now. Luckily, he enthusiastically high-fives me. His hand feels both firm and soft against mine.

"Were you coming back from a run when you found me embarrassing myself by falling off my bike like a toddler?" I ask.

"I was actually just heading out for a run. But there's nothing to be embarrassed about. You can't be a true Amsterdamer if you haven't fallen off your bike once or twice," he tells me with a reassuring smile.

"At this rate, I think I'm going for two digits," I smile back.

"I like your dimples," he says out of the blue. I feel a flattery growing in the pit of my stomach. I know my dimples are one of my best features, as many people have pointed out in the past. So, I don't know why this compliment is making me extra nervous.

"Thank you," I say.

I could sit here and talk to this guy for as long as possible. I'm drawn to him for some reason, even if an hour ago, I didn't even know he existed. But I know I shouldn't give in to whatever little infatuation is growing inside me. Getting closer to another man is the last thing I need right now.

"Um…I gotta go. I'm sure you also want to get back to your run," I say, getting up.

"You can stay. I don't mind missing my run." He looks disappointed, if I'm not reading too much into things.

"I can't. I have to go and…do things," I say, a bit flustered.

"Alright then. Can I give you a ride? I don't think it's a good idea for you to bike before your knee heals."

"No, but thank you. I live close by. I can walk." I'm already heading to the door, as though I have to run away to escape from whatever this energy is between us.

"Can I have your number?" he asks sheepishly. "I can show you around Amsterdam sometime."

"Um…I don't think that's a good idea. I just…I'm not in a good place at the moment. Sorry," I say, stuttering.

"No worries. I understand," he says, without trying to hide his disappointment.

I have to restrain myself from changing my mind and giving him my number. But this is not about him. This is about me protecting myself.

Chapter Six

I decide to spend the rest of the day at home. My attempt to be an adventurous traveler has been tragic. So it's better to stay in my safe haven where I don't face life-threatening accidents. Soon after I get home, Sophie texts me, telling me that she's stuck at work and apologizing for not being a good host and spending the day with me. Of course, she has nothing to apologize for. She's done more than enough, and one would think I'm an adult who can explore the city by myself. Well, we've seen how that went.

After lazing around watching TV and contemplating my life choices, I decide to take a shower before I have to start thinking about dinner. I haven't eaten anything substantial the whole day. I've lost my appetite for some reason, which is totally unlike me. If there is one thing one should know about me, it's that I can eat; I love to eat. But the last few days, I've been having a hard time building up an appetite. I guess emotional eating is not my thing. Noticing how my energy level is low, I promise myself to cook something good to fuel my body. But first, a shower.

The warm water feels so good on my bruised body that I audibly sigh. I let the water wash away the stress and tenseness from my body, at least, I imagine that's what it's doing, as I replay in my head the strange encounter with the good Samaritan. The encounter itself is not as strange as the effect it has on me—the way it left me all flustered and nervous.

I enjoy every last minute of the long shower. By the time I'm done, the steam has coated every surface, forming a dense fog on the mirror.

Right as I step out of the shower, I hear a door creak open and slow footsteps in the bedroom. I slowly shuffle to the bathroom door and press my ear to the door. I'm not imagining it. There is someone in my fucking bedroom, well, Sophie's bedroom. To further confirm my suspicion, I hear a drawer being opened.

Panic starts setting in. Did I leave the front door open? I don't think so. I distinctly remember locking it as I always do as soon as I get home. I know Sophie is not coming today, and as far as I know, she and Lucas are the only people who have the key to this apartment, aside from me. Considering Lucas is out of town, the person now loudly walking around my bedroom and rummaging through stuff has to be an intruder.

I remember with despair that I left my phone in the bedroom. I'm royally screwed. I look around the bathroom, searching for something to fend off the intruder with. The only thing that can be used as a weapon is the bathroom squeegee mop. I wrap a towel around my wet body and grab the mop. It's lightweight, but it'll have to do.

I slowly open the unlocked bathroom door and peek through. There is a tall man dressed in full black rummaging through the cabinet that still holds Sophie's things. He has his back to me. Maybe it's best to stay in the bathroom and wait it out. But I'd rather swing when he's still unsuspecting than wait for him to find me.

I slowly open the door wider and step into the bedroom. He's too focused on what he's doing to notice me. Maybe he has earbuds on. I have him right where I want him. I grip the mop with both hands, ready to strike.

Then, I run through the bedroom wielding the mop and smack him in the back with all my might before he registers what's happening.

"What the fuck!" he exclaims, turning around and lifting his hands to shield his face.

I swing again and smack him on his hands, screaming, "Get the hell out."

Then I see his face. It's none other than the good Samaritan himself, Daan. Did he follow me here? A fucking stalker. I thought he was a nice guy after the way he treated me when I was alone at his place. Who could have thought he would be a deranged creep?

All he manages to say is, "wait…wait" while retreating to the living room.

I chase him, still swinging my trusty weapon, the bathroom mop. Right in the middle of the hot chase, the towel I wrapped around my body loosens and drops to the floor. I am now naked in the middle of the living room, fighting a stalker with a squeegee mop. It's not lost on me that I look absolutely ridiculous. But I couldn't care less. I keep swinging, screaming, "Get out."

"I'm leaving, just stop," he says, looking at me between shielding his face. I don't give him time to take in what's happening. I swing again in the last attempt to drive him out of the door.

He catches the tip of the mop with his hand before it lands on his shoulder as I planned and says again, a little more firmly this time, "Stop, I'm going." He then opens the door with his free hand and leaves.

I slam the door as soon as his legs step out. Locking the door, I let out a breath for what seems like the first time since I left the bathroom. I look through the peephole. The coast is clear.

I rush to the bedroom to grab my phone and call the police. Right when I'm about to dial 112, I stop myself, unsure if this is considered an emergency in this country. The threat is already gone. I decide to call Sophie instead to ask how things work around here.

As soon as she picks up, I say, "Sophie, I know you're busy at work, but it's an emergency."

"What happened?" she exclaims. I can almost hear in her voice that she's getting ready to spring into action if I need her.

"Some stalker broke into the apartment, and I'm wondering if I should call the police," I say, my voice still shaking slightly.

"Wait, what?" Sophie screams.

I recount the events of the day as briefly as I can. I can hear Sophie audibly gasp when I tell her how I chased him away with a mop.

"You should definitely call the police. He knows where you live; he might come back. In the meantime, I'll ask Daan to come check on you. He lives nearby, and he can get there before I do," Sophie talks fast.

But I'm hung up on the name. "Who?" I ask incredulously.

"Daan, my brother," Sophie says matter-of-factly, as if this is the most obvious thing.

"The guy who broke into my apartment, his name is also Daan," I say, praying that this is just a coincidence.

"Oh my God, Gem. I asked my brother to grab some documents from my apartment and bring them to Zandvoort tomorrow. He has a key to the apartment," Sophie says.

"And you forgot to tell me that?" I exclaim.

"It totally slipped my mind. I also forgot to mention to him that you're now living in my place," Sophie responds with a sheepish voice. Of course, it's typical for Sophie to forget to mention such important details.

"Oh my God, Sophie. I knew your nonchalant attitude would get someone killed someday," I say, throwing myself on the couch. I'm partly relieved that he wasn't a stalker and partly mortified that I chased her brother out with a mop.

"Don't be dramatic," Sophie says, laughing. "Can you describe what the stalker slash intruder looks like just to make sure that it's my brother."

I do just that. I describe Daan in great detail. I'm able to do that because I was ogling him when he was bandaging me in his apartment. He took care of me, and I paid him back by chasing him with a mop naked like a crazy person. Talk about biting the hand that feeds you.

Then, Sophie starts laughing uncontrollably. "You beat up my brother with a bathroom mop. This is the most hilarious story ever. I'm never gonna let any of you forget about this," she says between giggles.

"You're the worst," I say, joining her in a laugh.

Then I hear Sophie's phone chiming.

"Wait, Daan is calling me. I'll talk to you later," she says in a rush.

"Please tell him how sorry I am," I plead.

"You can tell him yourself when you see him tomorrow." She hangs up before I can protest. What the fuck did I just do?

45

Chapter Seven

The next morning, Sophie calls to let me know that Daan will pick me up later to take me to Zandvoort for Sunday dinner at their parents' place. I protest. I don't know if I'm ready to see Daan one-on-one after the stunt I pulled last time. I still shudder in embarrassment when I replay in my head the scene of me chasing Daan with a mop, naked.

I'm even more surprised that he agreed to that. I'm pretty sure he hates my guts now, and I don't blame him. But I know Sophie can be convincing, and she must have worn him down. She says he'll be driving there anyway, and he lives close by, so it would be silly to take public transport when I have a ride. I reluctantly agree at the end.

I'm mortified to see Daan, but a part of me is glad that I get to see him before the dinner. It'll give me an opportunity to apologize and make things right instead of making the dinner awkward for both of us.

When the time comes, I put on a spring mini dress with yellow patterns and add a light gray trench coat. The weather is still chilly outside. I match the outfit with black ankle boots with short heels. I look at myself in the full-length mirror. My curly hair is freshly styled and bouncing on my shoulder, and my brown lipstick complements my caramel skin. My thick brows and long eyelashes add dimension to my round face. I smile at my reflection and see my dimples pop up. Daan likes my dimples—at least, he liked them before I attacked him like a total maniac. I'm not above using them to support my apology and get through to him.

When I return to the living room with my purse, I hear a knock on the door. Right on time. I take a deep breath, bracing myself for what's to come.

As soon as I open the door, Daan shoots up his hands in surrender. But I see the corner of his mouth twitching in a light smirk, which tells me that he's not serious. Maybe he thinks the whole thing is not a big deal. I really hope so.

"Ha-ha, funny," I say with a monotone, opening the door wide for him to come in.

"Are you sure you want me to come in?" he asks. I'm not sure if he's really scared or thinks I'm a total maniac.

"Yes, come in. I'm not crazy," I say with fake exasperation.

"The jury is still out on that," he mutters under his breath.

I close the door once he hesitantly enters the apartment. "Look, Daan. I'm so sorry about yesterday. I didn't know who you were. Sophie didn't mention you were coming, and I honestly thought you were a stalker or an intruder."

He listens to my apology, looking deeply into my eyes. I can't read his expression. I'm not sure if he's still mad.

"And you didn't help yourself by wearing a black hoodie," I add, flashing the dimples shamelessly.

"Yes, blame the victim," he says, his expression still unreadable.

"No, no! I'm joking. It's totally my fault. I shouldn't have jumped to a conclusion," I blabber.

An amused smile spreads over his face. "Relax. I'm joking. It's good that you protected yourself. If I'm a stalker or an intruder, I wouldn't dare to cross you again."

I sigh with relief. Thank God he's not mad. He might still think I'm crazy, but I can work with that.

"Plus, it's Sophie's fault. I know how forgetful my sister can be," he adds.

"Yes, let's all blame Sophie," I throw my friend under the bus without a second thought.

He laughs—a deep, growling laugh that shakes me to my core.

"Did I hurt you?" I ask. I've smacked him a few times with all my might. I've been wondering what damage I may have caused.

"Not really, your weapon was light. I'm more traumatized by you flashing me," he smirks.

Oh God, I just remember that Daan, Sophie's brother, has seen my fully naked body. I cover my face with my hands in embarrassment.

"Don't be embarrassed. It was a glorious scene. It definitely lightened the blow."

"Please, stop. I want you to delete that image from your brain," I hopelessly remark, peeking through my hands.

"I can't. It's imprinted in my brain forever," he laughs. He certainly is enjoying my mortification. I'm not one to be easily embarrassed. But flashing your fully naked body to your friend's brother the first day you meet him is next level.

I look at him, taking in his handsome face. I can't help but be drawn to his captivating laughter. He looks exceptionally good today in his blue Henley shirt, black jeans, and boots. The black overcoat he's added fits his tall, broad body like it's custom-made for him.

"Let's go before we're late for dinner," I say, trying to change the subject.

"Okay, let me first grab Sophie's document. I was rudely interrupted yesterday when I was doing that," he says, heading to the bedroom.

"You're not gonna let that go, right?"

"Nope. Do you mind?" he asks, pointing at the bedroom door.

I mentally scan the bedroom, trying to remember if there's any dirty underwear on the loose. I don't think so.

"No, you can go in."

The drive to Zandvoort is short, only around forty-five minutes from Amsterdam city center. Being in the car with Daan for that long isn't as awkward as I thought it would be. We have an easy banter that to anyone looking from outside, we don't look like strangers who only met the day before. It almost makes me forget that yesterday's events happened. Daan's easy smile and charm have taken the edge off and put me at ease.

Daan tells me about the neighborhoods and towns we pass on our drive with the articulation of a trained tour guide. Maybe I should've accepted when he offered to show me around the last time I was at his apartment. But I have a feeling that I won't be able to keep him just as a tour guide or a friend. I'm extremely drawn to him for a reason I can't explain.

Zandvoort is a beautiful coastal town known for its long beach stretching along the coast of the North Sea. It's a picturesque town with charming houses, bungalows, and resorts. Daan tells me that the town is also known for hosting an annual Formula One race. Zandvoort is quieter this time of the year as the weather is still not warm enough for a beach outing.

When we turn onto the street where Sophie and Daan's parents live, the houses start getting bigger and fancier until we reach a house that's more like a mansion. My mouth gapes in awe as Daan parks his Audi in front of a large white and gray mansion at the end of a long driveway. I knew their parents were wealthy, but I had no idea how wealthy. The three-story house is as majestic and gigantic as they come.

Daan doesn't register my surprise as he heads to the front door. Having grown up in this house, he probably doesn't even think about how big it is. I grew up on the Lower East Side in New York, sharing a tiny apartment with my mom. I couldn't even picture myself in this kind of house.

It makes me realize how different my world is from Sophie and Daan's. It's not surprising that Sophie is spontaneous and adventurous, while I'm a meticulous planner. In my world, planning helps you put a roof over your head and food on the table. If my mom hadn't planned every penny, I wouldn't have been able to go to school. If I hadn't planned my every move since childhood, I wouldn't have been able to attend college and then grad school on a full scholarship. People like me can't afford to be spontaneous.

But life doesn't always go as planned. According to my plan, I should've been in New York now, working as a corporate event coordinator by day and planning my small wedding with Justin by night. But look where I am now. Life gets to be spontaneous, and we just go along with it.

Sophie opens the door, trying to stifle a grin as soon as she sees us and not doing a good job at it.

"Good to see that you two haven't killed each other," she says, putting her arms around my shoulder and drawing me close.

"Give it time," Daan replies, moving past us and heading to the living room.

The inside of the house is as awe-inspiring as the exterior. It's decorated with expensive-looking furniture and artwork. The house is immaculate, every surface squeaky clean and shining. Kudos to the person who has to clean this house.

When we enter the living room, Sophie's mom and dad, Katherine and Maarten Peters, are sitting on the luxurious sofa, sipping wine.

Katherine gracefully rises from her seat, stretching her long hands for a hug. "Gemma, it's good to see you again."

She's tall and slender with golden blonde hair that matches her bright skin. It's clear she's not one to let her roots show under any circumstances. There are no lines or any other signs of aging on her face—thanks to Botox, I assume. She's dressed in a designer cocktail dress and heels. She looks like she's dressed for a fancy gala rather than a dinner in her own house. I give her a hug, mumbling greetings.

Maarten also embraces me in a bear hug. He's nothing like Katherine in appearance. Sporting a disheveled hair that's overdue for a haircut and a not-so-well-kept beard, he looks shabby next to her. It's evident that he didn't put much effort into his outfit either. Sophie must get her spontaneity and free spirit from him, while Katherine is quite uptight and proper. She's the CEO of their company and the house.

Sophie has mentioned before that her mom comes from a long line of wealthy businesspeople, while her dad comes from working-class parents. "They're so different in every way possible, yet they get along better than any two people I know. It's truly incredible," she's said. I can see what she meant—they move in sync like synchronized swimmers.

I met Katherine and Maarten in London when they came for Sophie's graduation. They took us to dinner at some fancy restaurant, and they probably spent what I spent in a whole year in London on just that one dinner.

I come to find out that for the Peters, Sunday dinner is not just a small family get-together. No, it's a whole feast with an extensive menu their private chef prepares. I stuff my face with various assortments of food items with zero shame. It's been days since I had a proper meal, and my appetite seems to return fully when I see the spread in front of me. I enjoy every course with enthusiasm that this table probably hasn't seen before. In addition to the food, the expensive wine keeps flowing, and I keep drinking.

Daan is sitting in front of me. He frequently glances in my direction until I meet his gaze. When our eyes lock, he breaks the contact, looking down at his plate as if he's nervous. Like I make him nervous. Then, I get nervous too. I have to stay away from this man. Why is my heart beating so fast in his presence when I haven't even started recovering from a heartbreak? I internally scold my heart for doing too much. *You're being extra for what?*

After dinner, Sophie takes Daan and me to the balcony overlooking the pool at the back of the house. Despite the slight chill outside, it's pleasant to sit here and sip wine.

Daan sits next to me, a bit too close for my comfort. If I move my leg even slightly to the left, I'll touch his leg. But I won't do that…hopefully.

Sophie takes the seat in front of us, scrolling on her tablet. She doesn't seem to notice my little predicament about how physically close her brother is to me. "There are still several wedding tasks that need to be done. From now on, you two are a team and will work together to check these tasks off my list," she says.

My heart jumps. I'm here losing my composure because he's sitting close to me, and she wants us to team up and work together? I'm in deep trouble.

"Why together?" I blurt out. "I mean, wouldn't it be easier and more efficient if each of us were assigned different tasks?" I'm partly concerned about efficiency, but primarily worried that spending so much time with Daan might not be a good idea.

"Efficient? Maybe. But effective? No. Gem, you're basically going to be my wedding planner. You'll make important decisions and help me organize everything. I trust your judgment and taste, and I won't be around as much. It's a busy time for me at work, and I also have upcoming business trips. That's where Daan comes in. He'll drive you around and assist you with everything. Plus, he speaks Dutch, so he can be your translator if needed," Sophie explains, shifting her gaze between me and Daan.

"You forgot a small detail. I have a job and a life," Daan interjects sarcastically.

Glancing between Daan and Sophie, I now understand why he looked so familiar when I first met him. Their resemblance is undeniable. The color of their hair and eyes is their main difference, appearance-wise. While Sophie has golden blonde hair, Daan's is dark blonde. Sophie's eyes are dark, a contrast to her otherwise light features, giving her an edgy look. Daan has blue eyes as clear as the California sky.

"Your job is more flexible than mine. Plus, you two can work around your schedule. And we all know you don't have a life other than going to work and playing football once a week," Sophie says, rolling her eyes.

In my peripheral vision, I see Daan shaking his head. It seems like he's decided to stop protesting and let her have her way. Like I said, Sophie is convincing.

"You play football?" I ask, stealing a glance at him. I can't help my curiosity; I want to know more about him.

"Yes," he says shortly.

"He had dreams about going pro when we were kids until he realized he sucked," Sophie chimes in, giggling.

Daan doesn't say anything. He just shakes his head again.

"What kind of football do you play?" I ask, not entirely sure why I'm probing. I'm supposed to be keeping my distance from him.

"The real kind. Not what you Americans call 'football'," he remarks pointedly.

"So, soccer?" I clarify.

"No, football. A game where you literally have to use your foot the entire time, unless you're a goalkeeper or when the ball is outside the field," he explains, seemingly heated now. For some reason, he has a very strong opinion about this, and it's amusing. So, I want to tease him further.

"Yeah, you're describing soccer," I say, attempting to keep a straight face.

He gives me an exasperated look. "What you Americans call football rarely involves using your foot. I refuse to call the real football 'soccer'," he emphasizes, putting air quotes around the word 'soccer.'

I burst out laughing, and he looks at me, confused. He must have thought we were having a serious debate.

I sense this isn't the first time he's had this discussion; he seems too exasperated, as if he's had this exact conversation multiple times before.

"How many times have you had this debate before?" I ask.

"I lived in the States for seven years. So, a lot," he sighs.

"For what it's worth, I agree with you. But it's hilarious that you have such a strong opinion about this," I manage to say between laughs.

Sophie joins in the laughter. "Daan has strong opinions about everything," she says.

"I just want things to make sense," he retorts.

"Okay, guys, back to my wedding planning," Sophie intervenes, returning her attention to her screen.

"Why do I need a translator again? I thought everyone here speaks English?" I ask. I've had no problem getting by with English in Amsterdam so far. Most people I've encountered here seem to be bilingual, if not multilingual.

"Not everyone, but most people do. Still, it would help to have someone who speaks Dutch with you to understand local intricacies. That's where Daan comes in," she explains.

Daan and I exchange looks, we both realizing that we're stuck with each other. I'm not sure if he likes the idea any more than I do. After chasing him around with a bathroom mop, I doubt he's thrilled about spending more time with me.

"These are the most important tasks you'll assist me with. First order of business, you two have to do the cake tasting and choose my wedding cake. I've already scheduled an appointment for Wednesday with the pastry chef who'll make my wedding cake."

"That's a crucial decision. Wouldn't you want to make that yourself?" I ask incredulously. I don't know any bride who would be willing to relinquish that level of control.

Sophie shakes her head. "You know I'm lactose intolerant."

"But you can have a lactose-free wedding cake," I suggest.

"Nope, I'm not going to make my guests miserable. I don't even like sweets that much. But my brother here has a sweet tooth, and he'd be more than happy to taste dozens of cakes," she says, looking at Daan.

"That's not wrong," Daan shrugs.

"Second order of business, flowers. I want to use mainly tulips to decorate the venue and for centerpieces."

"Could you be any more cliché? A Dutch wedding with tulips," Daan comments in a sarcastic tone.

"I don't care. Tulips are my favorite flowers, and that's the main reason I want to have my wedding this time of the year, during tulip season," Sophie says firmly. "And for this, two weeks from now, you two will go to Lisse to meet with a florist and decide on the flower arrangements for the wedding. I've already given her the vibe I'm going for, and she'll have options ready for you to choose from. Before you go, Daan will show you the wedding venue to help you decide on the best flower arrangements."

Daan and I both nod. At this point, there's no point resisting.

"Now, to the main event, other than the wedding, of course. A week before the wedding, we'll have the Peters versus Hofers sports tournament," Sophie squeals excitedly.

"What?" I ask, tilting my head to the side in confusion. This is news to me. I wonder if it's some kind of wedding tradition I don't know about.

"Yes. The bride's side, the Peters, and the groom's side, the Hofers, will compete in different games the whole day. We thought it's the best way for our extended family and friends to meet and get to know each other before the wedding," Sophie explains.

"How exciting!" I say. This is the best idea ever. I don't know why more weddings don't do that. It's certainly better than a rehearsal dinner or any other pre-wedding tradition.

"So, you two will help me organize that. Sima and Paige will also come from London for the tournament," she adds.

Sima and Paige are the other bridesmaids. We met them in London, and Sophie got closer to them when she lived there for a couple of years after we graduated, while I went back to the US. I've kept in touch with Sima, but not so much with Paige. I'm more than excited to see them again.

"What about Julia?" I ask. Julia is the only bridesmaid I haven't met yet, and Sophie has mentioned she lives in The Hague.

"She'll be there too. I'll introduce you to her before the tournament. By the way, she's Lucas's cousin. So, she'll be on his side of the family for the tournament."

"But she's your bridesmaid," I interject.

"Yeah, but the teams are formed based on family first. Daan is also one of the groomsmen, but he's playing on our side," Sophie tells me.

"I didn't know that," I say, looking at Daan.

"Yeah, Lucas is my friend, and that's how they met," he responds. Now I remember Sophie telling me about that when she first started dating Lucas.

Sophie sets down her tablet, signaling the end of the meeting. "I'll send you all the details and contact information you need. And for the next month, you two are my working elves."

Daan and I exchange another glance. I think I see a slight smirk forming at the corner of his mouth. He seems to be enjoying this or what's to come. Or maybe I'm reading too much into it.

None of us want to leave after finishing the wedding planning stuff. We sit there, enjoying the wine and each other's company. Sophie and I are close to being drunk after a couple of hours. Daan is still nursing his first glass after dinner, considering he'll be driving.

As Sophie is telling me about the time Daan drove his moped into a canal when he was fifteen, we hear the balcony door creak open. Lucas enters, holding a bouquet of flowers, and exclaims, "Verrassing!"

Sophie leaps from her seat, enveloping him in a warm embrace. It's evident that she's over the moon to see him.

Even at a time when my belief in love is a bit shaky, I still find this heartwarming. They remain in a tight embrace for what feels like several minutes before they finally pull apart.

"Babe, what are you doing here? I thought you were stuck in Budapest until Tuesday," she asks, gazing at him adoringly, her arms still wrapped around his neck.

"I finished work earlier than I expected and thought I'd surprise you." Lucas presents her with the flowers.

"These are beautiful. Thank you, baby," she says, planting a kiss on his lips.

"We're here too," Daan interjects pointedly, waving his hand as if Lucas hasn't noticed us.

Lucas comes over, first giving me a hug and then patting Daan on the shoulder. Sophie and Lucas settle in front of us, still joined at the hips.

"Good to see you, Gemma. And I'm very happy to hear that you'll be helping my very disorganized future wife with wedding planning," Lucas says, glancing at Sophie with a smile.

"I'm happy to help," I smile back.

"Sorry about Justin, by the way. I really thought he was better than that," he says with a more somber expression. He'd met Justin a couple of times when they visited us in New York.

"I did too," I respond quietly, my smile fading from my face. I've been trying so hard not to think about Justin or what he did. But hearing his name brings back that unpleasant memory of walking in on him and Mindy.

"Who is Justin?" Daan asks, oblivious to the situation.

"My ex-fiancé," I reply shortly, hoping he wouldn't ask follow-up questions. Justin is the last thing I want to talk about.

Daan looks deeply into my eyes for a few seconds and says nothing, which I'm grateful for. It's like he read my mind.

Lucas and Sophie are once again lost in each other's eyes, caressing each other's hair and stealing kisses in between whispers. I feel like Daan and I are third-wheeling them.

"Can we go?" I mouth to Daan. He nods.

Sophie and Lucas have recently bought and moved into a house in Zandvoort, not very far from Sophie's parents' house. I promise her to come and look at her house soon. But today, she needs to catch up with her fiancé, whom she clearly missed.

As we walk to his car, I tell Daan, "I want to go to the beach." I bet it's beautiful under the full moon.

He cocks his head and looks at me as if I'm insane. "Are you joking? The water is freezing."

"Please," I moan, tugging at his coat.

He shakes his head and relents, "It's your funeral."

When we get to the beach, it's empty, as one would expect at this time of the year and day. I take off my coat and shoes and place them on an abandoned lounge chair. I'm already feeling the cold in my bones, but I persevere.

"Are you seriously going to get in the water?" Daan asks in disbelief.

"I'm just going to dip my feet. You're not coming?"

"No, I'm sober enough to know that this is a bad idea."

"Your loss," I say, running to the shore.

As soon as my feet touch the water, I realize what Daan meant. The water is freezing. Like winter freezing, although it's spring. But I'm determined to go a little further. I don't want to chicken out and give Daan an opportunity to say, 'I told you so.'

I take a few steps deeper into the water until it gets closer to my knees. I don't need to go further.

"See? It's not that bad," I yell out to Daan.

Suddenly, a big wave crashes into me, sweeping me off my feet. I'm fully in the water now, the cold water stabbing every corner of my body.

I fumble to get up. I wish I could say I gracefully rise from the water, flipping my hair like a sexy surfer. But no, I clumsily clamber to my feet.

"Are you okay?" Daan calls out.

"I'm fine," I say, scrambling to shore.

As I approach him, he's not even trying to hide his 'I told you so' smirk. "How was it?"

"Exhilarating," I say loudly, trying to muster a convincing tone.

"I would've believed you if you could say that without your teeth chattering," he says smugly.

I don't like how he's standing there dry, looking so smug. Without even thinking, I lurch and wrap my hands around his waist in an attempt to get him wet.

"What are you doing?" he exclaims, surprised. But instead of pushing me away, he wraps his arms around me and rubs my back, trying to warm me. I get lost in his warm embrace. He is big, strong, and warm. While my body is shivering, a warmth flows inside me. I want to stay here.

"You're shaking," he says, pulling back and looking at me. His hands are still on my shoulder, but it's not the same as getting lost in his embrace.

"Take off your dress," he instructs.

"What?" I exclaim.

"Your dress is wet. You're better off just wearing your coat, and we can go to the car."

"Okay, turn around," I say.

He turns around, mumbling, "It's not like I haven't seen it before." I can hear the grin in his voice.

I take off my dress and bra, which is also soaking wet, and wrap my trench coat around my body.

"You can turn back around."

When he faces me again, he looks at the bra I'm holding in my hand pointedly.

"What? The padding holds more water than the dress," I retort defensively.

"I didn't say anything," he smirks.

I fumble with my shoes, trying to put them on, but my hands are shaking like a leaf. It seems like I'm getting colder and colder by the minute.

Daan steps in and takes my shoes, wet dress, and purse without saying a word. I just look at him, not knowing what he's doing. He then scoops me up and carries me with ease. I don't protest. Rather, I wrap my arms around his neck and settle in.

He walks to the car carrying me like I weigh nothing. His hands are warm against my back and the back of my thighs. My face is too close to his. I have an intrusive thought of hiding my face in the crook of his neck. And if I lean in a few inches, my lips can touch his.

I'm too focused on his face to realize we've reached the car. He must have felt me gawking at him because he glances at me briefly. I see his face flush as he catches me staring at his lips. Our eyes meet for a second, but I break eye contact. If I keep looking at him for one more second, I know I'd lose every ounce of control I have and lean in.

He doesn't put me down. Instead, he opens the car door, still carrying me, and deposits me in the passenger seat.

The drive back to Amsterdam is quieter than the drive to Zandvoort earlier. I don't know what he's thinking, but I'm replaying the moment we just had in my head. How close we were. How close I came to kissing him. Would he have kissed me back? Or would he have pushed me? But no need to dwell on this now. I shouldn't let myself get close to him like that again. A rebound is the last thing I need right now. Even if I decide to have a rebound, it can't be with Daan. He's my best friend's brother, and we'll be in each other's lives for a long time.

Chapter Eight

I am a morning person. I've always been that way. I often wake up around six, which gives me time to go for a run or hit the gym before work—except on the days I feel too lazy. So today, I wake up at six like clockwork, even if I have nothing to do or nowhere to go. Apparently, the jet lag didn't stick around for long. It amazes me how quickly my body adjusted to Central European time.

It's the first Monday since I lost my job. I lie in bed, staring at the ceiling. I feel purposeless. I didn't realize how much weight my work life carried until this moment. For the past four years, my routine revolved around my work schedule and Justin. Now that I've lost both, I honestly don't know what to do with myself.

My job gave me purpose and a sense of security, even if I didn't particularly enjoy or like it. I've been contemplating getting into an event planning business for a long time, but I didn't know where to start. Plus, I was terrified of not having a consistent source of income, I still am. Well, the universe might be forcing me to face my fear by taking away my job. But I'm not ready to see the bright side, if any, of the shitshow that is my life.

I wonder what Justin is doing right now. Is he spending the night with Mindy in our apartment—what used to be our apartment? I wouldn't put it past him. I picture him fast asleep next to Mindy. He's not a morning person like me. He likes to sleep in until he has to get up for work. He's one of those people who keep snoozing their alarms until they're almost late for work. That's why he's always rushing in the morning. It baffles me how it only takes him less than twenty minutes to get ready and rush out of the door.

I haven't heard back from Justin since the last time I saw him, the day I gave him the ring back. I got a Dutch phone number as soon as I got here and blocked him on all my socials. I don't know if he even tried to reach out. But even if he did, there's no way for him to reach me. I try to swat the Justin thought away. He doesn't deserve to live in my head rent-free.

Instead of dwelling on everything that's going wrong in my life, I decide to keep myself busy. I put on my running shorts and leave the house. The streets are relatively empty as it's still early. There are some early birds like me, jogging or walking their dogs. I run to Vondelpark—a beautiful public park in the center of Amsterdam.

The park is filled with lush greenery that can lift anyone's spirits. Spring flowers are beginning to bloom, painting every surface with cheerful colors. As I run through the park, I feel gratitude wash over me. I'm grateful that I get to escape my chaotic life in New York and be in this beautiful place. I'm grateful to friends like Sophie, who rush to my aid and pick me up whenever I fall.

After running a few kilometers in the park, I sit on the grass with my legs crossed under me, overlooking the small lake at the center. It's still cold outside, but I'm warmed up from my run. I take a deep breath and close my eyes. I remain in that position, doing a breathing exercise I learned on YouTube. It's supposed to help calm the mind down. Meditation isn't really my forte, although I understand its value. I can't seem to slow down my mind from racing a million miles an hour.

Amidst my futile attempt at meditation, I hear a deep voice calling my name. I'm surprised to hear my name in a city where no one knows me until I turn around and see Daan walking toward me. From the looks of it, he's also out for a run. He's wearing a black running outfit that fits his tall, lean body like a glove.

"Good morning," he says, looking down at me. He looks as handsome as ever with the early morning sun shining on his face. His hair is slightly damp from sweat. His arms, exposed from his running t-shirt, are toned and lean. The biceps stretching his sleeves show that running isn't the only exercise he does. The man is ripped.

"Morning," I say with a groggy voice. Although I'm a morning person, I don't like to be chatty and social for the first two hours I'm awake. I'm rather grumpy in the morning.

"Do you mind if I join you?" he asks.

I shake my head 'no'. He sits next to me, looking far ahead. We sit there like that for several minutes, neither of us saying a word.

"I didn't expect to see you here," I break the silence.

"This is my regular running route," he says. "I promise I'm not stalking you."

"No, no. I didn't think that," I say quickly before catching the smile at the corner of his mouth. I nudge his shoulder with mine. He glances at me with a smirk and nudges me back. I like the contact and wish for more until I remember why this is a bad idea.

"So, why are you really here, Gemma?" he asks, looking at me discerningly.

I glance back, my expression clouded with confusion. "At the park?"

"In Amsterdam."

I stay silent for a moment. I'm sure he can tell that I'm not here just to help Sophie plan her wedding. No one with a functioning life would abruptly move across the Atlantic to help a friend plan a wedding. But I don't have a functioning life at the moment.

"I lost my job and my fiancé on the same day," I say with a voice barely above a whisper.

"What happened?"

I can feel his gaze on my face, although I'm staring ahead at the water stretching before us.

"I got fired, and when I got home, I caught my fiancé with another woman on the bed we shared." My voice is cold and emotionless, which surprises even me. It's like I'm too exhausted, too broken to feel.

"That's terrible. I'm sorry," he says.

"Yeah. I didn't have anything to keep me in New York. When Sophie suggested I come here and help her with wedding planning to take my mind off things, I jumped at the opportunity. Well, it took a little convincing. But you know how convincing your sister can be." I smile faintly.

"Is it helping?" he asks. "Is being here taking your mind off things?"

I can feel him looking at me like he's trying to figure me out. Like he's trying to see what I'm really thinking. I feel a little exposed for some reason.

"I think so." I glance at him with a smile.

He meets my gaze with a somber expression. "Good. If you need someone to talk to, I'm also here."

This simple offer warms my heart, although I'm not sure if I'll take him up on it. I don't think he can be my confidant when I'm extremely and hopelessly attracted to him. And I can't act on the attraction. I just can't let myself go down that road. But I don't tell him that. I just nod and smile tightly.

***

After I return from my run, I feel significantly better. I take my trusty notebook and start planning the things I need and want to do while I'm here. I write down the museums, historical sites, and Dutch cities and towns I want to visit under different categories. I research each place, noting the opening hours, entry prices, and other relevant details. Before I know it, I have a detailed itinerary for the next month.

I don't care about what anyone says, but planning gives me purpose and direction. I like details, categories, and charts. I'm not ashamed to admit that a well-organized Excel sheet has an orgasmic effect on me. So it's not surprising that my morning grumpy mood has totally changed after spending hours working on my itinerary.

Meanwhile, I can't help but think about Daan. How he looked at me with those blue eyes of his when he said he was here for me. His words echo in my head, "If you need someone to talk to, I'm also here." I don't doubt for a second that he was sincere about it too. He meant every word he said.

Despite my best efforts, I can't keep this man out of my head. I don't know how I'd survive the next month of us working together. I want to know more about him for some reason.

So I let my curiosity get the best of me and decide to internet stalk him against my better judgment. I search his name on Instagram. He's the first Daan Peters that pops up. Thank God his account is not private. Requesting to follow him would defeat the whole purpose of secret online stalking.

He has several pictures on his Instagram page, mostly nature shots and pictures from the places he's visited. It seems like he's traveled all over the world. In the pictures where he's present, he looks effortlessly handsome and relaxed. I particularly stare at one of the pictures where he's looking straight into the camera for longer than I like to admit. He's giving a playful look with a crooked smile and sparkling eyes. I wonder who the person behind the camera is.

I scroll down to see if he's posted a picture of a girlfriend. I don't know why I need to know if he has a girlfriend. I'm not looking to date him, which I've reminded myself several times when my mind wonders about what it could be. But I let my curiosity get the best of me. From our interactions so far, there is nothing that indicates that he's in a relationship. I mean, he asked for my number the first day we met. Unless he's a sleazebag like Justin or he's in an open relationship, there is no reason for him to ask for my number if he has a girlfriend.

I don't see a picture of a woman other than those in big groups or his family members. But when I scroll down, I see a picture of him, Sophie, and a gorgeous brunette I don't recognize. The brunette and Daan are sitting very close, and they look extra cozy. I pinch the screen to zoom in on the picture and get a better look at this mystery woman. But to my absolute horror, I accidentally like the picture. I like a picture posted three years ago. One you have to scroll down a bunch to even see it.

Like any self-respecting internet stalker, I quickly unlike the picture and throw my phone away. I can't be trusted with this device. But the damage has already been done. I know he'll get a notification despite my attempt to remove my like. Now, it looks even more suspicious. What the heck did I just do? This is next-level stalker behavior. And of all the pictures, I liked the one where he was close to a woman. Could I be any more obvious?

I pray he's not one to check his Instagram notifications frequently, or my little blunder would be lost in the sea of notifications. I get my hopes up when I don't hear from Daan for the next two hours. I might have escaped unscathed this time.

But just when I start to relax, I receive a notification that Daan has followed me. After a few minutes, he DMs me.

Who is the stalker now? the text reads.

I'm royally busted.

I was just curious. I respond, still cringing on the inside.

Curious about what?

I don't have an answer for what I'm curious about other than the truth. Of course, I can't tell him the full truth. How do you tell a person that you're hopelessly attracted to them, and you want to know if they are dating someone else, even if you don't want to date them yourself?

Instead, I write, *Curious about what you do when you're not rescuing terrible bikers.*

Did you find your answer?

Part of it. Apparently, you're a global nomad. I text back.

I'm starting to relax now. I'm actually grinning at my phone like a fool.

That's not wrong. And I'm single if you're wondering about that.

He's on to me. But of course, I'm not going to admit that I'm curious about his dating or relationship status. *No, I was not wondering about that at all.*

Just in case.

As I'm thinking about what I should write in response, I receive another message. It's from Kelly, one of my friends I've been avoiding since I left New York. I met Kelly through Justin. They went to college together, and they stayed in touch afterward. Kelly and I hit it off the moment we were introduced and became quite close. She's closer to me than to Justin now, but I can't count on her loyalty if it comes down to choosing between him and me. Of course, I wouldn't ask her to choose. But I'm not sure she would choose me.

Most of Justin's friends are also my friends. When you date a person for four years, and that person is also your best friend, his friends become your friends, and your friends become his friends. Your lives morph together before you even realize it. I'm beginning to realize what a terrible idea that was. That's one of the reasons I've been avoiding my friends in New York since I broke up with Justin. I can't rant to them when I know Justin might also be doing the same and when I'm not sure that they would be supportive.

Kelly's message reads, *I've been trying your number. Where are you? I'm worried about you, Gem.*

75

Maybe I was wrong to question Kelly's loyalty.

Funny story, I'm in Amsterdam, and my US number is out of service. I respond.

Kelly's reply comes quickly. *What the heck are you doing in Amsterdam? I thought Sophie's wedding is a month away.*

It's a long story.

I'm not sure if she knew about Justin and my breakup. He would've immediately blabbered to our friends if it wasn't him who cheated with one of our friends. But maybe he didn't tell them as he was clearly in the wrong. If there's one thing I know about Justin, he really doesn't like situations or facts that make him look bad. He deeply cares about what others think about him. The cheating definitely doesn't put him in a good light.

Call me now!!! Kelly's text reads like a loud scream.

I can't keep avoiding my friends. Plus, I have nothing to hide or to be ashamed of. It's Justin who has something to be embarrassed about. I'm sure Kelly would agree with me about that, which is why I decide to call her right away.

Kelly picks up on the first ring. I brace for the barrage of questions I know she'll throw at me.

"Hey, Kelly," I say, trying to muster a cheerful tone.

"Thank God, you're alive. Why are you in Amsterdam?" she exclaims with her usual exaggerated tone. I picture her gesticulating dramatically as she often does when she talks.

"Didn't you hear what happened with Justin?"

"He told me you found out about him and Mindy. I'm sorry, Gem." She doesn't sound surprised by the fact that Justin and Mindy are sleeping together. In fact, the only news to her seems to be the fact that I found out.

"Wait, did you know?" I ask.

The line on the other side falls silent. Kelly is not one to stop talking. But now she doesn't seem to find the words.

"Kelly?"

"Look, I found out a couple of months ago, and they promised they'll break it off," she says with an apologetic tone.

"How could you hide that from me? I thought you were my friend." My voice cracks a little.

"I'm your friend. But it was not my place to tell. I didn't want to ruin what you and Justin have." Her tone is a mix of pleading and annoyance. What does she have to be annoyed about? She's the one in the wrong here.

I'm surprised that Kelly knew about this juicy gossip and kept it to herself. Everyone knows she can't keep a secret if her life depended on it. But she kept Justin and Mindy's secret, at least from me—the person who needed to know the most. That tells me everything I need to know. There's no questioning where her loyalty lies.

"Now, why are you in Amsterdam?" she asks again when I don't respond.

"I'm helping Sophie plan her wedding," I simply say. I'm still reeling from the fact that she knew about Justin and Mindy and didn't bother to tell me.

"What about your job?"

I contemplate whether I should tell her about losing my job. I don't feel like confiding in her after what I just found out. But there's no point in keeping that to myself. She's nosy enough to ask around and find out herself.

"I lost my job."

"Oh Gem, I'm so sorry."

I don't like the pity in her voice. "It's okay, I need a break anyway. I'm enjoying my time here," I say. I don't know if I'm trying to convince her or myself.

"So, what are you thinking?"

"About what?"

"About Justin...your engagement?" Kelly says.

I'm confused. We just talked about what happened. "What's there to think about? We broke up; there is no engagement."

"Come on, Gem. Do you really want to throw away what Justin and you have? You're like the best couple I know."

I can't believe what I'm hearing. How is this on me? I'm seriously getting annoyed now.

"He threw away what we had when he decided to sleep with our mutual friend," I say through gritted teeth.

"I know, he messed up. But he said it's just sex. Even Mindy knows that."

I scoff to complement my eye-rolling that she can't see. Am I supposed to be grateful that it's just sex and that it doesn't mean anything? He broke my trust. That means everything. I can't believe Kelly doesn't get that.

"Look, no relationship is perfect. If ninety percent of the relationship is good, you have to overlook the ten percent that's not working. That's why some of your heroines decided to forgive their cheating husbands," she adds.

I'm sure steam is coming out of my ears at this point. If I stay on this phone call for one more minute, I'm gonna say something I might regret or, even worse, spontaneously combust.

"It's over between Justin and me…" I start.

"You two love each other," she interrupts me.

"Kelly, there is no point in talking about this. It's over. I gotta go now," I say firmly and hang up the phone without waiting for a response.

I'm now convinced that my decision to avoid my friends is indeed right. I'm grateful to Sophie more than ever now. Not only because she gets me and supports me no matter what, but also because she took me out of a situation and a place where, apparently, I have no support.

Chapter Nine

After my little online stalking incident, I'm embarrassed to see Daan again. I keep embarrassing myself around him for some godforsaken reason. He probably thinks I'm a total weirdo. But I can't hide from him even if I want to. Today is Wednesday, and we're scheduled for cake tasting. I nervously pace around the apartment while waiting for Daan.

I hope he doesn't mention the Instagram debacle. Because if he does, I don't have a convincing explanation for why I liked the picture from three years ago, a picture with a woman at that. Plus, I'm a horrible liar as is, and I know I won't be able to lie under the scrutiny of those deep blue eyes. They tend to have a disarming effect on me. And I obviously can't tell him the truth when I know the truth doesn't make a whole lot of sense even in my head. Especially when the truth involves admitting that I'm extremely attracted to him.

I hear a knock at the door while I'm having a full-blown internal dialogue with myself. When I open the door, Daan is standing there, wearing a long black overcoat that pronounces his tall figure.

"Hey," he says, pulling me for a hug, which catches me off guard. I awkwardly wrap my arms around him. He smells nice too. The woody and earthy undertones of his cologne or aftershave are captivating. I find myself sinking deeper into the hug.

"You look nice," he says as we pull apart.

I look down at my ankle-length flowery dress with a side slit as if I'm not the one who chose my outfit. "Thank you. You look nice too."

"Ready to devour dozens of wedding cake samples?" he grins ear to ear. He definitely seems excited about the prospect of tasting cakes. I'm grateful that he doesn't mention the stalking incident.

The cake design studio Sophie picked is a luxurious studio located in Amsterdam Zuid. This place is any sweet-loving person's dreamland. It smells like sugar, cinnamon, and whatever other concoctions bakers use. Baking is not my forte. I tried to bake banana bread a couple of times in the past, and I managed to accomplish the impossible—my banana bread came out burned on the outside and totally raw on the inside. To be fair, I completely ignored the recipe and measurements and eyeballed everything. That has never failed me with savory. But with sweets, it's a different story. I still have hope though. One day, I'll bake something edible. Not a very high bar, I know. But I gotta start somewhere.

We are greeted with champagne and a warm welcome by staff gleaming with perfectly trained customer service smiles. People treat you like royalty when you pay enough. Sophie and Lucas are paying the premium, while we enjoy the royal treatment.

When we are seated to start the consultation and tasting, I take my tablet out of my bag and open the Excel sheet

I prepared in advance. I've already called Sophie to ask what vibe she and Lucas are going for. But she didn't really care. She just said we need to choose something that looks good and pleases the crowd. She's putting too much faith in my judgment, and I need to take this seriously. Hence, the meticulously organized Excel sheet.

"What is that?" Daan asks, tilting his head, a light crease forming between his eyebrows.

"This is the Excel sheet I prepared to help us choose the best cake flavor and design. We rate each cake based on flavor, texture, looks, and public appeal. The highest-scoring cake will win. Each rating category has different elements, as you can see here," I hold up the tablet to his face. "So, make sure you take all these into account when you judge the cakes we taste," I say with a straight face.

He looks at me incredulously as if trying to gauge whether or not I'm joking. I certainly am not. I don't joke when it comes to planning. And this is a perfectly reasonable system for choosing the best cake.

"Wow, how are you and Sophie friends?" he says, his mouth gaping with surprise just so slightly.

"That's something I ask myself frequently."

The first cake we taste is vanilla buttercream. Daan eagerly shoves a spoonful of cake in his mouth and groans with delight. He really has a sweet tooth. If you think this man's speaking voice is deep, you should hear his groan. It reverberates in a way that quickens my heartbeat against my will.

He goes for another scoop. "This is so good."

"Slow down, tiger. We have ten more samples to taste," I say, taking note on my Excel sheet.

We go through all the wedding cake samples, Daan making all the happy noises and me prodding him to describe and rate the taste. After intense deliberation, we narrow down to two choices: vanilla buttercream and lemon flavor. We think both are generally liked by most people. We decide not to go for some of the exotic flavor combinations we've tasted. While we both like them, they might be polarizing.

After a long discussion and reference to my trusty Excel sheet, we land on the lemon cake. It has more of a spring vibe to it, which perfectly fits the wedding aesthetics. Meanwhile, I choose a beautiful six-tier cake design that can be customized to accommodate the wedding theme and aesthetic. Daan gives me full control on that.

Daan keeps going back to the samples he's most liked and eating extra spoonfuls. I'm surprised by how much cake he can eat. I've struggled even with the first round of tasting. Finally, he leans back on his chair like he's exhausted from all the cake tasting.

"I think I'm in a cake coma if that's a thing," he says, his eyes nearly closing.

He looks so vulnerable in that position, his tall body leaning back on the chair, appearing all limp. I have an intrusive thought that I can't resist. I scoop a good amount of buttercream frosting with my fingers and draw a goatee on his chin.

He doesn't resist; he just says, "That's very mature."

He really is in a cake coma. It's as if his limps are not functioning to even swipe the cake off his face. I snap a picture of him sprawled on the chair with a cake goatee, giggling. I'm not helping my case concerning his sarcastic comment about my level of maturity. But I'm kind of proud of my artwork.

I send the picture to Sophie with a message, *Your brother is passed out from cake overdose, and I'm drawing on his face like mean frat boys.*

At least you're not chasing him around with a mop this time. He should be grateful. Sophie's response comes quickly, which makes me chuckle.

Daan remains in the same position, sporting his cake-goatee. After I'm done having my little fun moment, I lean in and swipe the cake-goatee from his chin with my fingers. My thumb lightly grazes the corner of his lower lip, which sends shivers all over my body and makes my heart jump a little. Without even thinking, I lick the buttercream frosting off my fingers.

When I look up at Daan, his face is flushed, and he has this strange look in his eyes I can't quite place. I can't believe I just licked a cake off his face. I used my fingers, but still. The whole thing seems very intimate and, might I say, a tad bit sexual.

He's still looking at me, especially at my lips. "You have frosting on your lips," he says with a hoarse voice.

I lick my lips, trying to get the frosting. Using my hand or a napkin doesn't even cross my mind. I'm too flustered to be able to think logically.

"Here," he says, swiping the corner of my mouth with his thumb. My lips quiver a little, and his fingers linger briefly before he clears his throat and pulls away. But I can still feel his finger on my skin. My face is so hot that I can almost feel my cheeks burning. What is this man doing to me?

Chapter Ten

I'm bored out of my mind. I know I shouldn't be bored when I'm in this beautiful and charming place with so much to do and see. And I've been doing just that—going out and exploring the city. But I don't feel like doing anything today. I'm having one of those days when even getting out of bed feels like an insurmountable chore. I stay horizontal as long as I can, mindlessly staring at the ceiling.

Normally, I wouldn't mind staying in bed, reading, or watching TV when I have one of those days. But not today. I'm feeling restless at the same time, as though I can't stay put if my life depended on it. I think about texting Sophie and asking her to come over. But I don't want to bother her more than I already have. She has a company to run, for God's sake. Unlike me, who is jobless, fiancéless, and borderline homeless.

My brain starts to spiral. The negative self-talk is getting overwhelming. I don't want to sit here and drown in self-pity. I need to do something, even if I have no desire to do anything. But I also don't want to stay home and dwell. It's not lost on me that I'm running in circles.

I jump in the shower just to give myself something to do. I take a long, luxurious shower in an attempt to wash away all the bad vibes from my body. It helps a bit. But the boredom doesn't go away.

Just when I'm contemplating going out, my phone dings, alerting me to an incoming text message. It's Daan. We exchanged numbers after Sophie forced us to work together to help with the wedding. We've been texting each other sporadically since then. So, I'm not surprised when I see the text.

Left work early. You want company?

My face floods with a smile as I read the text. It's like my fairy guardian has told Daan how I'm feeling and what I need more than anything at this very moment. I don't even care if I vowed to stay away from Daan, or any man for that matter. I need company more than anything to keep me from spiraling. And from what I know so far, Daan is a great company.

Yes. Come over. I'll order pizza. I text back.

Daan and I haven't hung out alone outside of the wedding planning tasks. I felt a bit nervous about having him in my place alone. Did I mention that I'm hopelessly attracted to him?

My phone pings again. *Great. Will bring beer.*

Daan arrives with a pack of beer not long after. He has a business-casual look going on, which makes me stare at him for an extra-long moment. He's wearing a navy-blue shirt with black khaki pants and holding his black overcoat in one hand. I catch a glimpse of his firm chest through the few unbuttoned buttons of his shirt. I briefly imagine what it would feel like to run my fingers over his chest but immediately force myself to stop thinking about that and focus on inhaling my pizza.

"What do you wanna do?" I ask after we've eaten the pizza and settled on the couch.

He gets up and walks to the shelf with a stack of board games in the corner. Sophie and Lucas are board game enthusiasts, and they have an extensive collection that they haven't moved to their new place yet. I don't even know what most of these board games are.

"Do you play chess?" Daan asks.

"Yeah, but I can't say I'm good," I respond.

He grabs the chessboard and walks back, placing it between us on the couch. I sit facing him with my legs crossed underneath me.

After we both make our first few moves, I say, "Two truths and a lie. Go!"

"What?" he asks, moving his knight to target my bishop.

I laugh at the confused expression on his face. "Tell me two truths and a lie about you, and I'll guess the lie."

"Okay... um... I've traveled to all continents except Antarctica; I am an avid skydiver; and finally, I've been arrested for indecent exposure," he says, smiling mischievously.

I don't have to think about this much. The lie seems evident. There's no way he exposed himself in public. That doesn't sound like him at all. "This is easy. The lie is you've been arrested for indecent exposure."

He starts cracking up. "Wrong. That's actually true."

"What? Daan Peters! Do you have a troubling dark past?" I ask, my eyes wide and my mouth gaping in disbelief.

He doesn't stop laughing. "I blame your country for it."

"I need to hear the full story," I say. His laughter is infectious. I start laughing too, even though I don't know the full story.

"It happened when I was a freshman in college. I just moved to the US and became friends with these two guys from Florida. They were wild in every sense of the term, always pulling crazy stunts and daring each other to do crazy stuff. So, one night, they insisted on going skinny-dipping after getting drunk at a party. I refused, but they were so insistent. I finally relented, although I was fully aware that it was a bad idea. It turned out, it was a prank on me, a stupid frat hazing. Guess what these assholes did?"

"Oh my God, they took off with your clothes?" I chime in, truly mortified on his behalf.

"Yes, they left me naked in the cold. At first, I thought they'd come back after a few minutes. But no, they left. I couldn't stay in the water; I was extremely cold. So, I started to walk around the lake naked, hoping to find them hiding somewhere close. Instead, some people called the police, and I was taken to the station."

"That's awful. I hate those assholes," I say, my expression a mix of amusement and anger. Who does that to their friend?

"I know. I stayed the fuck away from them after that. Fortunately, the police officers took pity on me because I was a 'naïve international student who was new to the country.' They didn't press charges. I was basically released with a slap on the wrist and some stern words from the older police officer."

"So if that's a truth, what is the lie?" I ask, moving one of my last pawns to make the move I should've made twenty minutes ago. But Daan's story is so captivating that it takes my focus away from the game.

"The lie is that I'm an avid skydiver. I actually have a bit of fear of heights, and I have never done skydiving, nor do I plan on doing it," he says, capturing my rook with his bishop. He'll win in just a few more moves if I don't pull some trick out of my sleeve. But I have no trick up my sleeve.

"Now, your turn," he says.

"Okay, let me think…I was a national spelling bee champion in middle school; I had sex for the first time when I was twenty-two; and I talk in my sleep sometimes." I list my facts, moving my surviving rook to target his bishop, which is guarding his king. He backs his knight, predicting my move. If

I capture the bishop, he'll take my rook with his knight, which is the only helpful piece I have left.

"The lie is you didn't have sex until twenty-two," he says flashing me a shy smile.

"No. That's actually true. I was a late bloomer."

"Was it worth the wait?" He smirks.

I blush. I can't help thinking about what a first time with Daan would feel like. What his heaviness on top of me would feel like. It would certainly be better than my actual first time. "Not really. I'm glad I waited. But my first time was not great."

"What went wrong?" he asks, looking down at the chessboard.

"I just didn't feel comfortable. It just didn't feel as good as…you know…when doing it on my own," I say, staring directly at him. But he doesn't meet my gaze.

I see Daan's face flush when I mention doing it on my own. Maybe he's picturing what that looks like. For some reason, I like the fact that I make him nervous. He clears his throat in what seems like an attempt to calm himself.

"So what's the lie?" he asks.

"That I was a spelling bee champion. I was in the national bee competition, but I didn't make the finals. 'Octonocular' was the word that got me. I still remember that sucker," I say, begrudgingly reminiscing about my spelling bee days.

"What the hell is that?" Daan asks, raising his eyebrow.

"Having eight eyes," I respond, laughing at his reaction.

"But you made it to the semifinals of the national competition. That's still super impressive."

Daan is impressed by me. That makes me happy.

"Another round," I say, making my last attempt to save my vulnerable king.

"Alright," he says, pausing to think. "I have a nickname for you that you don't know about; I've never broken anything before; and checkmate." He surrounds my king in all rounds and declares his win. That's one truth.

"The lie is the first one; I don't think you have a nickname for me," I respond.

I honestly can't think of a nickname Daan can have for me that I don't know about. We don't have our lives intertwined enough for him to use a nickname when I'm not around. Does he even talk or think about me when I'm not around?

He flashes me his mischievous smile. "Wrong. I call you 'the naked ninja' behind your back." He bursts out laughing.

"Daan…," I poke him in his ribs with my leg. "You talk about me behind my back? To whom?"

He holds my foot to restrain me from poking him and sets it on his lap. "Mostly just to my horse. She's a good listener."

"You have a horse? Who are you?" I exclaim dramatically. To think you know someone.

He laughs. I notice the weight of his hand resting casually on my leg. This minor contact makes my heartbeat hitch.

"My family owns a ranch, and they gave me a horse for my sixteenth birthday. Miss Brenda has been in my life for sixteen years now," he says.

"Your horse's name is Brenda?" I start cracking up.

"It's Miss Brenda. The name actually fits her very well. She's moody and has a mad attitude." He laughs with me, his gaze fixed on my face.

"Did I tell you that I like your dimples?" he says reflexively, as if he didn't mean to say it out loud.

I stare into his eyes. "You did, actually."

"They're gorgeous," he says and averts his gaze. I like these moments where I see a glimpse of shyness in Daan's otherwise confident personality.

He absentmindedly trails his fingers on my leg resting on his lap. A surge of warmth travels through my body, reaching deep within my core. I fear he might sense the sudden change in my body temperature through my skin.

"I really want to meet Miss Brenda. She sounds like my kind of person… I mean, animal," I say, attempting to ease the tension building between us, or at least the tension I'm feeling.

"Let's go, then," he says, placing my leg back on the couch and getting up. A sudden chill replaces the warmth.

"Now?"

"Yes, do you have somewhere else to be?" He holds out his hand. I take it and let him pull me up.

"You didn't tell me what the lie is," I say as we walk to his car. He's still holding my hand.

"The lie is that I never broke anything. I broke my arm when I was in high school."

"Let me guess, you fell off Miss Brenda?" I speculate.

"Actually, yes. Nice guess," he says, smiling down at me.

Once we're settled on the road, Daan glances at me and says, "Your turn."

"I once got drunk and sent a particularly harsh email to my professor in college; I have a belly button piercing; and I got fired for the first time in my entire life recently," I say.

"Let's see…" he says, lost in thought. "I know you have a belly button piercing, so that's easily true."

I glare at him, leaning forward from my seat. "How did you know that?"

I see a smirk forming at the corner of his mouth. "You forget I have already seen you fully naked."

"But that was for a brief moment. I didn't think you would notice my piercing," I respond.

"Oh, I noticed, alright," he says pointedly.

Why did I bring up a body piercing? Now I'm reminded of my embarrassing moment with Daan, one of my embarrassing moments, I should say. Not even a week ago, I was chasing Daan around Sophie's apartment, naked, wielding a bathroom mop.

"The other two are tough to choose from," he interrupts my train of thought. "I think the lie is that you got drunk and sent a harsh email to your professor. I can't see you doing that; you seem like someone who took school very seriously."

"I did," I say. Daan's read on me is extremely accurate. "I was a total nerd, still am, and I took school very seriously. I'd be mortified if I did something like that."

"By the same logic, I think you're good at your job and everything you do. So it's unlikely that you have been fired multiple times," he adds.

"Well, being good at my job didn't save me from getting fired," I say. Even I can hear the bitterness in my tone.

I don't know why I brought up this issue. This is supposed to be a fun game.

"Can I ask why you got fired?" he asks, his tone turning somber.

"Apparently, the company is shifting its focus, and my expertise is not needed anymore," I say, imitating my former boss, Michael's voice.

The farm ranch is located a few kilometers outside of Amsterdam. At this point, it doesn't surprise me that his family owns a ranch. I've closely seen how wealthy they are. Not just regular wealthy, but the kind that gives a horse to their kids for their birthday. The kind that sends their kids to the US and the UK for college, paying full tuition in advance. The kind where the kids graduate to fat trust funds and management positions at the family business. A generational wealth.

Daan gives me a brief tour of the ranch and takes me to the barn where Miss Brenda is. Miss Brenda is a magnificent black horse. She stands tall and graceful, her ebony coat glistening. She's truly majestic.

Daan gently strokes her neck, shoulder, and back, talking to her as if she can listen to him. I cautiously hang next to him without stretching my hand to touch her.

"Hey, Miss Brenda, this is my friend, Gemma, you know her as 'the naked ninja'," he says, scratching her at the withers.

Miss Brenda doesn't even bother to look at me. She's ignoring me like I'm not even in the room.

"Miss Brenda here is the boss of this place, and she's known for giving mean side eyes," he adds, looking at her adoringly.

Just on cue, Miss Brenda gives me a side-eye, which makes me laugh. "She's my spirit animal. I be side-eyeing my way through life too," I say.

"You do more than side-eyeing…naked ninja," he chuckles, looking at me mischievously.

I lightly punch his arm, which garners me another side-eye from Miss Brenda. She doesn't seem to like me attacking her friend. I quickly retract my hand apologetically.

"See, even now, you're choosing violence," Daan exclaims, holding his arm as if he's really injured.

"You can pet her, by the way," he says.

I hesitate. "Are you sure? She doesn't seem to like me."

"She likes you. She just has a perpetual resting bitch face. Don't you, Miss Brenda?"

I pet her silky ebony coat, emulating what Daan did. It turns out Miss Brenda has a calming effect on me. She doesn't seem to mind me either. Maybe she's just tolerating me, but I can work with that.

"Do you want to ride one of the other horses?" Daan asks me. "Miss Brenda is a bit difficult to handle for someone who doesn't know her."

"No. I actually have never done this before," I say, a bit embarrassed about my lack of experience. I don't tell him the fact that this is the first time I got this close to a horse, unless you count the time I was almost knocked down by one of those New York City carriages in Central Park.

"You have never done horseback riding?" he asks, sounding surprised.

"No. I grew up in New York City, and the closest I got to riding a horse is when my dad used to put me on his back and gallop around the living room when I was five," I respond.

I surprise myself by casually mentioning my dad in a conversation. I never talk about him. Not only because it's been so long since I saw him that his memory has greatly faded, but also because I made an intentional choice not to talk or think about him a long time ago.

"But I want to watch you ride," I say, brushing off the unpleasant memory. The memory itself is not unpleasant, but thinking about my dad is.

"I can't ride in these clothes. I'll go inside and change. You can walk around and look at the other horses if you like." He heads out of the barn and into the building attached to it.

After a while, he emerges wearing a riding attire. I have to say he looks phenomenal in his tight riding pants and boots.

He saddles Miss Brenda with utmost care. She obeys him diligently. It's like they have a special language between the two of them. It's adorable to watch.

I stand leaning on the riding ring fence while Daan rides. It's nice to see him in his natural element, looking all determined and in control while guiding the horse around the riding ring. Miss Brenda majestically walks, trots, canters, and gallops following his guidance. I watch the beautiful scene play out in front of me with a wide smile on my face.

"You have to try it, Gem. You can just be on the horse, and I can guide it for you," he says, settling next to me after he's done.

"I don't know…" I hesitate.

I'm scared of falling off the horse or being thrown back by the horse. It's hard to try new skills as an adult when you're too aware of the dangers and too self-conscious of failure. Especially for someone like me who even falls off a bike, trying to ride a horse for the first time might be tempting fate too much.

"You'll be fine, I promise. And I'll be next to you the whole time," he reassures me, as if he can read my fear from my face. I hesitantly agree to give it a try.

He places the saddle, and whatever other gears one needs for riding on a smaller and friendlier-looking horse. Miss Brenda is too moody to be ridden by strangers. She even gives me a side-eye that says, 'don't even think about it' when I walk past her. "I wouldn't even dare, ma'am," I whisper to her.

Daan helps me up, and I settle on the back of the horse, adrenaline taking over my nervousness. He explains to me what I need to do like a passionate teacher. When I don't understand some of the jargon of riding, I ask him to explain it like I'm five. So he does. He patiently guides me until I get the hang of it.

Despite my initial hesitation, it actually feels amazing to be on the back of a horse. I feel like I'm on top of the world. It feels exhilarating. As he promised, Daan doesn't leave my side when I try to guide the horse to walk around the ring. By the end of the day, my restless and bored feelings have been replaced by pure joy. And I can't deny that Daan's company has a lot to do with it.

Chapter Eleven

I scan the bar until I spot Sophie sitting at the table in the corner, scrolling on her phone. Weaving through the Saturday night bar crowd, I make my way to her table. Sophie doesn't look up until I'm standing right in front of her.

"How did you manage to score this huge table in this crowded bar?" I ask, leaning in to hug her.

She puts the back of her hand under her chin and bats her eyelashes. "I used my charm."

I throw myself into the chair and pick up the drink menu. I badly need a drink.

"I love the cake you chose, by the way. That's why I trust you with these things. You have an eye for it," Sophie says.

I've sent her pictures with a detailed description of our selection process.

"I'm glad you like it. Helping you with the wedding planning is actually making me reconsider my event planning business idea. I feel like I need to bite the bullet and go for it," I say, still browsing the menu.

"You should totally go for it. You would be amazing at it. I'm telling you, you have a knack for these things," she responds excitedly. Sophie is the ultimate hype woman.

"Maybe I will. Now, help me choose a drink," I say. I'm a bit confused by the menu. I've never seen a beer list as long as this one, not even in the pubs in London.

"This place is known for its beer selection. I recommend one of the Belgian beers. What do you prefer, a bitter or lighter beer? Low or high alcohol content?" she asks, scanning the menu herself.

"Lighter taste and high alcohol content," I respond without hesitation.

"Gem came to play…I like it. I have just the perfect beer for you. I'll go to the bar and order. No one is going to notice us here," she says, already getting up.

She comes back, holding a bottle of beer and a glass after a few minutes. I look at the label on the back of the bottle before pouring, noticing the above-average alcohol content. This will do.

"Have you talked to Justin since you left New York?" Sophie asks, her furrowed brows displaying her concern.

"No. My US number is inactive, and I've blocked him on everything. The last thing I want is to hear from him," I say, taking a big swig of my beer.

"That's not a bad idea. You had your closure when you found him fucking another woman," she says, with a clear disgust in her voice.

I nod. "You know who I talked to instead? Kelly. She made me call her a few days ago. She apparently can't see a reason why I should break it off with Justin. She said cheating is an imperfection I can overlook if the other aspect of the relationship is good."

Sophie rolls her eyes. "That's a load of BS. Trust is the most important part of any relationship. Breaking trust is not a minor imperfection. The way some women keep lowering the bar for men is astounding. You deserve the absolute best, and you don't need to overlook shitty behavior."

I smile at her adoringly. This is one of the reasons I love Sophie. She doesn't take nonsense from anyone.

Just then, a tall brunette walks over, beaming from ear to ear. She looks familiar, like I've seen her somewhere before, but I don't know where. She hugs Sophie, exchanging greetings in Dutch.

"Julia, this is my friend Gemma," Sophie says, shifting her gaze between Julia and me. Ah, Julia, the other bridesmaid.

Julia flashes me her beautiful smile and stretches her hand, "Nice to meet you, Gemma. I've heard a lot about you."

"Nice to meet you too," I say, taking the hand she's holding out.

I now recognize why she looks familiar. She's the woman in Daan's Instagram picture—the one I accidentally liked, exposing myself as a stalker. She's even more beautiful in person than in her picture. She has big green eyes and a chiseled face with high cheekbones. She can cut Dutch cheese with those jawlines.

"I love your hair. It's so…big," Julia says, taking a seat beside Sophie.

"Thank you?" I say, unsure if it's a compliment or a dig. I assume the former. I don't care what anyone says; I'm having a good hair day. My curls are popping, no frizzy strands in sight.

We sit there discussing wedding shenanigans. Sophie is the most laid-back bride ever. She just wants to have a fun day with her friends and family. I've never heard her use the term 'my big day' to describe her wedding. She often refers to her wedding as 'the party,' which is a blasphemy of the highest level to those who take weddings too seriously. But I like Sophie's version of what a wedding means—a fun party where people come together to celebrate love and family. It certainly takes away the pressure of having a perfect day.

A while later, Daan, Lucas, and Floris—another one of the groomsmen—join us. Floris is much shorter than Daan and Lucas, who tower over everyone. He's probably of average height, but he looks tiny when standing next to these two giants.

My heart lurches when I see Daan, and he doesn't help the situation by sitting next to me. Too close that our legs bump against each other a few times. It doesn't seem to affect him the way it does me. *Is it just me, or is it hot in here?* I think to myself as I feel my face burning.

"So Gemma, how does it feel to beat up this jerk with a broom... or was it a mop?" Floris asks just moments after we meet. Apparently, he doesn't have a filter.

"It was a mop. And it feels empowering," I say, glancing at Daan, who shakes his head in disapproval. But I see the corner of his lips twitch with a smile.

"You've become my favorite person since I heard that story," Floris beams at me.

"Wait, what's the story?" Julia asks, looking around the table.

"You haven't heard? You have to hear this. So, it was Saturday evening, the city was buzzing with the weekend energy..." Floris begins telling the story, leaning on the table, as if he were there when it happened.

"Dude, you weren't even there," Daan interrupts.

"Let him tell the story; I like this version," I say.

Daan shrugs, glancing at me.

Floris tells the story of how I chased Daan with a mop, adding his own embellishments. According to his version, Daan begged for his life, and the only reason I let him go was because I felt sorry for him.

Everyone at the table is wheezing with laughter.

Even Daan is cracking up next to me. Then he leans in and whispers in my ear, "Should I tell them that you were fully naked half the time?"

"Don't you dare," I whisper back.

"Why not? You losing your towel in the middle of the hot chase is the best part of the story," he teases, smirking. "I think everyone would enjoy hearing about the belly button ring too."

"Stop," I say, lightly nudging his shoulder.

It makes me happy to know that Daan hasn't told his friends about the most embarrassing part of the story. In a weird way, I feel like he's protecting me. So, I flash him a grateful smile.

When I look up, Julia is glaring daggers at me for a reason I can't understand. I sit up as if I am on alert.

"So let me get this straight. You were staying at her apartment, and you didn't stop to think that maybe he was someone who knew Sophie before you attacked him?" Julia asks, as if that's the most unhinged behavior she's ever heard of. Her tone is confrontational.

"I know how it sounds. But I didn't know that anyone other than Lucas and Sophie had the key to the apartment. I was scared, to be honest, and I panicked," I say, trying not to match her confrontational tone. She already thinks I'm unreasonable, and I don't need to give her another reason.

"I get that, but that's a bit aggressive, don't you think? Do you always overreact like that?" she asks, looking straight into my eyes. The animosity in her tone is palpable. I just don't understand why.

I don't respond; I just glare at her in disbelief. Responding might give her more ammunition to label me as "aggressive." Everyone at the table falls silent, sensing the change in the mood.

"To be fair, it was my fault. I forgot to tell Gem that Daan would be stopping by to grab some things from the apartment," Sophie intervenes, clearly trying to defuse the situation.

"I actually think her reaction was warranted. She was alone in a new apartment in a city she was not familiar with. When she saw a stranger in her bedroom, her instinct was to defend herself. If I were an intruder, as she assumed, her reaction was effective. I wouldn't have dared to try anything," Daan says firmly.

The others also nod in agreement. Julia keeps her mouth shut after that.

"Thank you," I mouth to him. He winks at me in response. I can feel Julia glaring at us; I'm sure she's seen our inaudible interaction. I don't know why she's acting like this. Does she like him? Have they dated before? But even if that's the case, there is no reason for her to be frosty toward me. Daan is just my friend.

"I'll get another beer. Does anyone want anything?" I ask. I want to get away from the table for a minute more than I need a drink. They all shake their heads 'no'.

I head to the bar, navigating through a slew of people crowding the bar. "What can I get for you?" the bartender with long hair and sleeve tattoos peering from his black t-shirt asks.

I rack my brain to remember the name of the beer Sophie ordered for me. "I forgot the name of the beer I just had. Something Tripel?" I say apologetically.

The bartender winks at me with an understanding and starts listing the names of different beers so fast that I can't hear half of it.

"That one," I interject excitedly when he mentions something that roughly sounds like the name of the beer I've had and hope that it's the right one.

"Coming right up."

As I'm waiting for my drink, I hear a voice behind me say, "Hi." Turning around, I see Julia standing right in front of me.

"I didn't mean to offend you earlier. I tend to be too straightforward sometimes," she says with a neutral expression.

If she thinks she's apologizing, she's doing a horrible job at it. I don't hear an apology in her statement. Then again, she might not even intend to apologize.

"It's fine," I match her neutral expression.

The bartender hands me my beer.

"You and Daan seem to be close," she says right when I'm about to leave.

"No," I retort, a bit too defensively than I intended. "I mean, we're helping Sophie with the wedding stuff, but we're not close-close," I add, hoping she'll get the hint that nothing is going on between Daan and me. If that's what she's worried about, she can rest her pitchfork. I return to the table without waiting for her response.

The rest of the night at the bar is uneventful for the most part. Floris dominates the conversation, making everyone laugh by telling ludicrous stories, which I assume he's taken creative liberty in telling.

"This place is getting boring. Let's go clubbing," Julia suggests out of the blue.

"I second that," Floris says extra enthusiastically.

Sophie furrows her brows in disapproval. "Clubbing at our age? We're too old for that shit."

"You make us sound like we're geriatrics. We're just a group of late twenties and early thirties folks," Floris responds.

"I don't know, guys. I don't want to spend my night fending off college kids trying to grind on me," Sophie says, looking disgusted by the thought.

"I have a perfect place where we can avoid that. It's a classier place, and the hefty entry fee will keep college kids away," Floris persists.

"I'm in," I say. Sophie looks at me incredulously, as if saying, 'I'm supposed to be the spontaneous one.' I seem to be beating her at her own game.

"Me too," Daan says immediately after hearing my response.

"Fine, let's go clubbing," Sophie relents, although she doesn't sound convinced. And we all know Lucas will follow wherever she goes.

"Come on, it'd be fun. Like the old times," I say, pulling Sophie to her feet.

Daan and Julia walk ahead of us, and Floris and Lucas follow behind. Floris has said the club is not far from here. So we're all walking.

Julia links her arm with Daan's and says something to him. He bursts out laughing. They walk with their arms linked the whole way, talking and laughing. They have this comfortable familiarity. I feel a little pinch in the pit of my stomach.

"What is their deal?" I ask Sophie, pointing my chin to Daan and Julia walking in front of us.

"They used to date, like seriously date. They were together for three years. He was so heartbroken when she broke it off. But they remained friends against all odds. I didn't think it was a good idea for them to be friends when he was still hung up on her. I guess Daan still wants to have her in his life, even if not as he hoped," Sophie says, looking straight ahead.

I feel a pang of jealousy, although I don't understand why. There's nothing between Daan and me. It's evident that Julia has his heart. Their breakup wasn't his choice. As if I need more reasons not to act on my attraction to Daan, it's clear he's still in love with his ex. One should not go down that road even for a rebound.

"I honestly thought they would end up together. We all expected them to get married at some point. They were all over each other, so in love. Then all of a sudden, she ended things," Sophie continues, oblivious to how her words are effecting me.

Chapter Twelve

The club we enter is indeed classy and upscale. Seating booths are scattered across the vast space, and surprisingly, the dance floor isn't as packed as I expected for a Saturday night.

We gather around a larger booth in a corner, far from the dance floor. We order cocktails, and Floris insists on buying shots for everyone, which we accept. Everyone is on a different level of drunk at this point.

When the DJ starts playing the nineties and 2000s R&B jams, I can't resist pulling Sophie onto the dance floor. Floris joins us while the rest hang back. We dance, singing along with some of our favorite hits. Although my first impression of Julia is rocky, I'm grateful to her for suggesting this. I haven't felt this carefree in so long. I let my hair down and dance the night away, literally and figuratively.

After dancing until I'm huffing and puffing, I head to the bar to get another drink. While I'm waiting for the bartender to notice me, a guy with a fancy-looking blazer approaches me, flashing a charming smile. He has a nice set of teeth, and the corners of his eyes crinkle when he smiles, which is adorable. His thick dark hair and well-trimmed beard curve his tanned face. The man is hot, I must say.

"Hey, would you do me an honor of letting me buy you a drink?" he asks with an Italian accent.

"How can I say no when you ask like that?" I flash him the dimples.

"What's your poison?"

"Moscow mule," I say, dragging my words. I'm on the higher level of tipsy.

He places our drink order, Moscow mule for me, and whiskey on the rocks for himself. "I must admit I was looking at you while you were dancing. You're gorgeous," he says, his eyes scanning my face and my body. The man exudes an effortless confidence that can disarm anyone.

"Thank you. You have beautiful eyes," I say, flirting back. Apparently, the alcohol has taken away all my inhibitions.

He looks deep into my eyes. "Not more beautiful than yours."

"I have to hand it to you. You're smooth," I chuckle.

He throws his head back and laughs, like I said the most hilarious thing ever. I'm not sure if this is also part of his game.

"I have to pull all the stops, just for you. I was hoping to convince you to dance with me."

"That's not a big ask," I respond.

"Maybe dancing will lead to other things," he says, looking at my lips.

Just then, I see a familiar figure towering over me. "Here you are. I've been looking all over for you, babe," Daan says, putting an arm around my shoulder. I didn't see him coming. It all happens out of the blue and so fast. I also can't seem to stop my heart from lurching when he touches me.

"Who is your friend?" he asks, looking at my flirting buddy.

His hand is resting on my lower back now. He's holding me like he has done this countless times before. Like we are a couple in a loving relationship.

"Sorry, I didn't know you have a boyfriend," the fancy blazer guy says, retreating back like he's trying to fade into the background.

As soon as the charming Italian man is out of earshot, I turn to Daan with an incredulous look. He slowly removes his hand from my waist. I wouldn't have minded if his hand stayed where it was to be honest.

"What was that about?" I ask.

"You're welcome," he says, grinning.

"For what? For chasing away the pleasant company I was enjoying?" I tilt my head and glare at him. Part of me is glad that he's here with me. Another part of me urges me to stay away from him.

When it comes to Daan, it's like my head and heart are at odds. Logically, I know I shouldn't get too close to him. But there's an irresistible attraction that keeps pulling me toward him no matter how hard I try to resist.

"I was trying to rescue you," he says.

"Rescue me from what?"

"From where I was standing, it looked like he was bothering you."

"Are you sure? From where I'm standing, it looks like you got jealous when you see another man showing me attention," I say, looking squarely into his eyes. Maybe it's the liquid courage, but my filter is nowhere to be found.

He looks down at me straight into my eyes, matching my stare. "Maybe," he says.

I don't have a retort. I was not expecting him to agree with me. I down my drink and look at him daringly.

I then grab his hand and pull him to the dance floor. "Since you chased my potential dance partner away, you have to dance with me."

He doesn't resist. I notice that Sophie and Floris have retired to the booth. It's only the two of us from our group.

Daan dances better than I expected. For some reason, I thought he wouldn't have such an easy command on his tall and shredded body. It turns out, he can move in a way that can make anyone hot and bothered including yours truly. I can't help being captivated by how sexy his every movement is.

While I'm shamelessly thirsting over Daan, the beat drops to a slower R&B. Following the intimate beat, I take a step forward to get closer to him. As if he understands what's on my mind, he pulls me by my waist and slams me against his body. My heart skips a beat. *Damn you, heart. Be cool.*

Our bodies are pressed against each other. Thigh to thigh, breast to chest—actually lower chest. I notice how perfectly we fit together, despite our glaring height difference. Without even thinking, I'm body rolling and grinding against him. We move in sync, swaying our hips together.

I feel a warmth flowing in my body and a tingle between my legs. I don't think I can resist if he presses me against the wall and kisses me. I wouldn't even resist if he wraps my legs around him and…

"What are you thinking?" he asks, interrupting my thirsty train of thought.

We're still swaying to the beat of the music.

"Nothing," I say. My face burns with embarrassment, like he can see my lustful thoughts written all over my face. What is this man doing to me?

He leans down toward me, his face so close to mine. "Were you planning to dance with that guy like this?"

"No, this is just for you," I say hoarsely. I'm sure he can barely hear my voice above the music blasting in the club.

"I'm glad. I wouldn't have liked seeing you dance like this with another man," he says, leaning in closer. His warm breath brushes against my skin, sending chills all over my body.

If he leans in one more time, our lips will touch. I don't think I'd mind that. Actually, I'd very much like that. It's like the world has stopped, and we are the only two people in this place. We're so focused on each other that we don't see the other people sharing the dance floor.

Just then, I hear Julia's chipper voice. "Can I join you guys?"

We pull apart and make a space for a three-way dance, which brings me back to reality. The reality of our situation. A love triangle is the last thing I want to be a part of.

I dance for a few more minutes just not to be rude to Julia before excusing myself. "I'm gonna get back to the booth. I'm all danced out," I say, looking at Daan. I think I see what looks like a disappointment wash over his face.

Chapter Thirteen

I'm waiting for Daan to come pick me up. He's showing me the wedding venue. I haven't seen him since our close call last Saturday, and it's Monday today. Part of me is relieved that we didn't kiss. It would've complicated things, and I'm trying to stay away from 'complicated.'

But I can't deny that I'm excited to see Daan again. I haven't stopped thinking about him for some reason. I've been replaying Saturday night in my head non-stop: how close he was to me, how his body felt against mine, the way his lips parted just inches away from mine. I can still feel his hot breath against my face. Would he have kissed me if Julia didn't interrupt us?

I'm awakened from my daydream when my phone buzzes on the table. It's a US number that I don't recognize. Not many people from the US know my Dutch number. Who could it be?

Swiping the screen, I hold the phone to my ear warily. "Hello?"

"Gem, it's me. Please don't hang up." It's Justin. I don't know who gave him my new number. It must be that leaky-mouth Kelly. Fucking Kelly.

"What do you want?" I hiss.

"I want to tell you that...I want you back. I miss you so much. You know I love you," he pleads, sounding desperate.

But I don't let it get to me. I used to find it extremely hard to say 'no' to Justin. He has this wounded, sad puppy look when he wants something, which he leisurely utilizes to get his way. That won't work on me anymore. Not only because I don't see his face now, but also because that face has been deceiving me for the past however long he's been sleeping with Mindy.

"You should've thought about that before you decided to fuck our friend," I say with disgust in my voice. Doesn't he realize that I will never trust him again? Love is not enough when trust is lost.

"I know I messed up. I just need a second chance to prove that what we have is worth trying to fix. Anything you want, Gem, I'll do it. Couples therapy, starting from dating again or from being friends...just name it," he pleads.

"I can't trust you, Justin. Nothing can fix that," I say, my voice lower now, sounding cold and resigned.

"Please, Gem. I can't lose you," his voice breaks a little.

"You already did," I whisper.

I hear him sigh deeply, as if he's deflated. "Okay, can we at least talk from time to time? No expectations."

"No, please don't call me again," I respond firmly.

"How could you do this to me?" he asks, his voice carrying a sharper edge.

I did this? Is he really putting the blame on me? I feel rage consuming me. "What? You're the one who did this. What part of this do you not understand?"

"You can't possibly blame me for everything. Yes, I made a mistake, but you're not perfect either," he says defensively.

I'm lost for words. Is he seriously mad at me after what he did? He deceived me and snuck behind my back not just once or twice, but for years. The fact that he even has the audacity to say what he's saying is beyond me.

"I know I'm not perfect. But I'm not the one who threw away a four-year-long relationship like it means nothing," I exclaim.

My anger is mixed with sadness, hurt, and the feeling of betrayal. My eyes burn with tears that are threatening to fall, but I don't let them. I can't give him the satisfaction of knowing that he made me cry.

"Everything has to always be your way. You don't compromise and stray from the plan even when it means so much to me. You took me for granted, Gem. You never try anymore," he says.

I don't respond. I just let him push the dagger deeper.

He continues, "You know when Mindy and I first slept together? It was the weekend I asked you to go to that music festival with me. But it didn't fit your preset plan, so you said 'no,' even though you knew I really wanted to go. You know who abandoned all her plans to go with me? Mindy. You pushed me into Mindy's arms."

My tears start falling. I didn't think Justin would hurt me more than he did when I caught him with Mindy. But he manages to do it. He not only cheats on me with our mutual friend but blames me for it. 'I made him cheat. I pushed him into Mindy's arms.' If this isn't closure, something I didn't even realize I needed, I don't know what is.

My tears are streaming down my face, but I'm calm, and my voice is cold. "Justin, never talk to me again."

I hang up the phone and collapse on the couch, sobbing. All the emotions I've been suppressing since I left New York flood me like an avalanche.

***

I met Justin four years ago at a random coffee shop. Our first meeting really was a meet-cute. I used to play this game with myself where I gave made-up names to a person taking my coffee order. I even made up backstories for the name and tried to have fun with it.

So that day, I was Justina, a hot divorcee who hated everything and everyone. Being in Justina's mind was helping me calm my nerves. I was nervous because I had an interview in thirty minutes—an interview for the job I was just fired from. And I needed coffee and a distraction.

I was people-watching and thinking about how Justina would think that everyone rushing for work in the morning was despicable when I heard the barista call out, "Triple shot cappuccino for Justina."

I hurried to the counter and grabbed the Styrofoam cup at the same time as this tall guy wearing a blazer and thick-framed glasses. He had this sexy professor look going on.

"Excuse me, are you also Justin?" he said, pointing at the name written on the cup.

I glanced at the name; it indeed said 'Justin.' "No, I'm Justina. I must have misheard the name," I said apologetically.

He must have seen the disappointment on my face because he said, "You know what? Take it. I'll wait for Justina's order."

"Are you sure?" I asked, touched by his gesture.

He nodded, looking intensely at me.

"Oh, thank you so much." I grabbed the coffee and bolted out, rushing to my interview. I had time, but knowing myself, I'd get lost trying to find the office where my interview was scheduled. So I had to account for that.

My interview went very well. I had an easy interaction with the hiring committee, including Michael, who turned out to be my direct boss. I'd even go as far as saying that they loved me. So, I was beaming with a smile when I got into the elevator after I left the interview room. After just two floors down, the elevator stopped, and the sexy professor stepped in. Apparently, he worked in the same building.

"Hey, you're the coffee bandit," he said with a cheerful grin.

"You offered," I smiled back.

"Justina, right?" he asked.

"No. Actually, I'm Gemma."

He looked at me in confusion.

"I do this thing where I give fake names at coffee shops. It's just a little game I play with myself," I explained awkwardly.

"I like that. Nice to meet you, Gemma. I'm still Justin."

"Nice to meet you, Justin."

"Now you've got to buy me lunch after taking my coffee and running away." He winked at me.

It was a bit early for lunch. But I'm in a cheerful spirit after nailing my interview. What the hell? We spent the entire afternoon together—lunch turned into a long walk and then a movie. When he walked me home that day, we had our first kiss, and the rest is history.

It didn't take long for us to fall deeply in love. It felt like we were meant to be, or at least I thought so at the time.

We had an easy banter, shared many interests, and got along quite well. Although our upbringing was different, we came from similar economic backgrounds and neither of us had an easy path in life.

Justin was the first man I fully trusted. Before I met him, I always had my guard up, which was one of the reasons why I didn't date much when I was younger. But Justin made me comfortable, and he got me in all the ways that mattered to me. He was supportive and stuck by my side in all the ups and downs in the past four years.

That's why I was utterly surprised and hurt when he cheated on me. That was the last thing I expected from Justin. Even more so, it broke me when he blamed me for cheating. What I heard was I wasn't attentive enough, accommodating enough, exciting enough. I wasn't enough.

Chapter Fourteen

I can't stop crying. I haven't cried like this in a long time. I can feel my eyes getting heavy and my face swelling, but my tears don't stop falling. I'm completely broken. It's not just Justin. Everything that went wrong in the past and the uncertainty about my future hit me like a brick. All the emotions I've refused to deal with take over me at once. I feel like I'm having a nervous breakdown.

Just then, I hear a knock on the door. I realize in horror that it must be Daan. I don't want him to see me like this. I don't even feel comfortable crying in front of my close friends, let alone my friend's brother, whom I'm hopelessly attracted to. I often deal with my emotions in private and face the world with a smile. I've always been like that.

But I can't ignore Daan when we have an appointment. I've already texted him, telling him that I'm home waiting for him. He's going to think something is wrong if I don't respond. I wipe my eyes with my sleeve and head to the door.

His face falls as soon as he sees my puffy face and red eyes. I didn't get a chance to look at myself in the mirror, but I don't need to see my face to know that I look horrible.

"Gem, what's wrong?" he asks. His concern is palpable in his voice.

That breaks the unstable dam I've built to stop my tears. My tears break every barrier and wash over my face.

I walk back to the couch without answering him. My knees feel too weak to stand. Daan follows me and sits next to me. I sob uncontrollably, my body shaking despite my effort to control myself. I'm having a full-on mental breakdown in front of Daan.

"Hey, hey…" he says, wrapping his arms around me and holding me against his chest. He doesn't say anything else. He just caresses my hair and lets me cry all over him. After what feels like ages, my sobbing starts to subside. I start to calm down.

"What happened?" he asks, still holding me close to his chest.

"Justin just called, and he basically told me that I'm the reason he cheated," I sniffle.

Daan has a calming presence. I can feel myself getting relaxed against his chest. I can stay like this forever.

"Justin is an idiot," he says with no hesitation.

"But you don't know him," I say, lifting my head from his chest and looking at his face. I feel a smile creeping onto my face when he says that, but I'm too sad to fully smile.

He cups my face, wiping my tears with his thumbs. "He cheated on you. I don't need to know more."

"Justin is an idiot," I laugh while still sniffling. It's like when the sun comes out while it's still raining outside. A smile takes over my cloudy, tear-streaked face.

"Hey, the dimples are back," he says cheerfully and pokes at my dimples, grinning.

I put my hand on his chest, feeling the dampness from my tears. "Sorry, I snotted all over your shirt."

"Anytime," he murmurs, putting his hand on top of mine and holding it on his chest.

I can feel his heart beating fast. My heart also matches his rhythm, beating fast like I just climbed a flight of stairs. We stare at each other for a few seconds, and I feel the energy change between us.

I need to move, but I'm frozen in place. Lost in Daan's kind eyes, every fiber in my body wants to get closer to him. It's not just me; I also notice the changes on his face. I see his jaw clench and his eyes dart to my lips just so slightly.

"Um… I'll clean up, and we can go," I say to break the tension.

He doesn't pull away immediately. He holds me for a moment, as if he hasn't registered what I just said. As if he doesn't want to let go. Then he softly says, "Yeah," and pulls away.

The wedding venue is a huge mansion that resembles a medieval castle. It sits in the middle of a large acre of land covered with well-trimmed plants and surrounded by trees. It's as picturesque as it gets. They must be spending a fortune renting this whole venue for three days. Yes, they're renting the entire place for the whole weekend, Friday to Sunday. Sophie has told me that her parents and Lucas's parents, who are also equally wealthy, are paying for the wedding. So everything is extravagant and over the top.

The ceremony will take place in a large hall that looks like a church, (I was told it's not; I asked). There is another, less traditional-looking hall for the reception. It is surrounded by large glass windows, which gives it an outdoorsy feel. It also has a huge terrace overlooking the beautiful greenery. I can't wait to see the wedding photos that come from this place.

The venue also has a bridal suite and rooms for close family members and the wedding party. We'll be spending three days on this all-inclusive getaway.

I bombard the venue staff with countless questions about logistics, space for catering, the open bar, and decorations. Many of the details have already been taken care of by the wedding planner, who started the process before she quit. But I just want to make sure that everything is in order. I inspect every surface closely, taking notes and pictures, thinking about flower arrangements that work best with the place, a task that Sophie entrusted me with.

After I finish, I join Daan, who is standing outside, leaning on the terrace railing. He seems lost in thought, staring far ahead into the lush greenery.

"Do you also want to get married in this kind of venue? I mean, if you want to get married in the first place," I ask, taking the place next to him.

"I definitely want to get married. But a big wedding is just not my thing. I prefer to have an intimate ceremony at sunset by the beach or lake," he responds, glancing at me.

"That sounds romantic."

"How about you?" he asks.

The question brings back the memory of the wedding I was planning for myself. Justin didn't really care about the wedding, so I had complete creative control. "The wedding I was planning before I broke off my engagement was small. It was actually not far off from what you just described."

"Wow, maybe we should get married then," he laughs.

"Yeah, right," I scoff. But I entertain the idea in my head. What it would be like to be married to Daan. To spend every night with him, to wake up next to him.

"Let me show you something." He interrupts my train of thought, already going down the short steps of the terrace.

I don't move right away.

"G, come on," he calls out, holding out his hand. It's the first time he calls me 'G,' and I like it. It feels intimate for some reason. Everyone calls me Gem or Gemma, and I'm secretly happy that he has a special nickname for me, well, other than 'the naked ninja.'

Taking the hand he stretched out, I follow him down. He tugs me along the narrow clearing to the woods surrounding the property.

"Where are we going?" I ask.

"You'll see when we get there."

After walking in the woods for a few minutes, we arrive at a clearing surrounded by trees. A small pond lies on the far side, and a small deck stretches out toward it. It really feels like something from the movies.

"Wow, this is beautiful," I say, taking in my surroundings.

"I prefer this over the big extravagant mansion."

"I can see it. The couple will be on the deck, and the guests will sit on this side," I say, gesturing to the green clearing we are standing on.

He holds my hand again and tugs me to the deck. When we reach the end, he looks at me and asks, "So, the couple will be right here?"

"Yes, they can exchange vows here," I say excitedly, my event planner side kicking in. I can clearly picture the whole ceremony in my head. "The person officiating the wedding can stand right there," I gesture with my chin.

Caught up with planning an imaginary wedding, it takes me a while to realize that we are standing like a couple ready to get married. Holding hands and staring at each other.

I let go of his hands and sit on the deck with my legs dangling over the water. "Have you ever come close to proposing?"

"Once," he says, sitting next to me.

"To Julia?"

He looks at me, surprised. "How did you know?"

I don't look at him. I'm staring far ahead, but I can feel his questioning gaze on me. "Sophie mentioned you dated."

"Yeah, we were together for three years. I was planning to propose to her before we broke up." His voice lowers when he mentions breaking up with Julia.

"How did you plan to propose?" I ask. I love hearing about proposal stories, even the cringy public proposals.

"I was planning to take her to Santorini. We had our first trip as a couple there, and I knew it was one of her favorite destinations. I was thinking about booking one of those private villas overlooking the sea and proposing there at sunset. Cheesy, right?" he says, releasing a breathy laugh.

"No, that's cute."

He laughs genuinely. "Cute? I was going for romantic."

"It's romantic," I say, glancing at him.

My mind drifts back to my own proposal story. Justin proposed in Times Square like a common fool. It was humiliating. I thought he knew that I hated public proposals.

132

But I loved him and wanted to marry him, so I said "yes" even if I was cringing inside. Then, I insisted on going home right away to escape the judging eyes of New Yorkers and tourists crowding Times Square. Some clapped, bless their hearts, but it didn't help with my embarrassment. I always wanted an intimate, meaningful proposal, which I subtly hinted to Justin whenever we talked about getting married. So, a proposal at a private villa in Santorini sounds like a dream.

"Do you mind if I ask why you broke up?" I ask, staring out across the length of the pond.

"She said she didn't love me anymore. I thought everything was fine. Then, one day, she woke up and decided that she didn't love me anymore." His voice is clouded with sadness.

I can't imagine what it feels like for a person you've spent years with and planned a future with to suddenly say they don't love you anymore. There's nothing you can do to fix it. You can't change how a person feels, and you can't blame them for how they feel either. It must be devastating. It's evident that he still loves Julia. I wonder if he would go back to her if she says she loves him too.

"So, how's dating after Julia?" I ask, smiling at him to try to lighten the mood.

He doesn't smile back. "I haven't been dating since then, to be honest. I needed some time to myself."

"Wait, how long has it been?" I ask, surprised.

"Almost a year. I recently met a beautiful woman who made me excited about dating again. But she rejected me before I could even ask her out," he says, smirking.

"Why did she reject you?" I honestly don't see a reason why anyone would reject Daan without even giving him a chance. He's good-looking, tall, and extremely nice and considerate. He is the full package.

"Let me ask her and get back to you," he responds, looking at me pointedly.

"What?" I exclaim, confused.

He laughs at my confusion. "Why did you say 'no' when I asked you for your number on the day we met?"

Oh, the beautiful woman who made him excited about dating again is me. "I broke up with Justin two days before we met. I was not in a good place to even entertain the idea of dating."

I see understanding wash over his face. He flashes me a playful smile. "I get that. I guess it was just bad timing."

Now I know Daan is attracted to me too. But our circumstances haven't changed. I'm still going through a breakup and working through my feelings. And he is probably still in love with his ex. It's bad timing, indeed.

Chapter Fifteen

These days, I'm embracing the slow and soft life I've been gifted, albeit against my will. If I'm staying in this beautiful city without a job, I might as well take advantage of it. My once constant need for exhaustive to-do lists and tightly packed schedules is gradually fading away.

I start my mornings leisurely—sleeping in or reading in bed until my stomach grumbles for breakfast. I then head to one of the cozy coffee shops in the city. Not the coffee shops that sell weed, but the coffee shops that sell actual coffee, although I admit I've also visited the former a couple of times. I take my time enjoying my morning cup of coffee and some form of pastry.

I spend my afternoons going to museums or one of the smaller cities near Amsterdam. For instance, yesterday I went to Utrecht, a city just forty kilometers south of Amsterdam. Utrecht is the smaller and quieter version of Amsterdam; that's the best way I can describe it. It's lined with some of the most beautiful canals I've ever seen and charming streets. I walked around the city for over three hours, immersing myself in my surroundings.

One of the perks of being in a small country like the Netherlands is that you can practically take a day trip to any part of the country, thanks to the easily accessible public transport. It's one of the things I envy about Europe: easy access to public services. Granted, I haven't been to all parts of Europe, but the places I've been to so far have easily accessible and relatively affordable public services, at least compared to the US, where capitalism creeps into every aspect of life. In many parts of the US, getting around without a car is close to impossible. Education and healthcare are so expensive that they are the main sources of financial strain for many US residents. The tuition fee my friends here pay is close to nothing.

In addition to exploring charming cities and towns, I'm also attempting to learn Dutch; 'attempting' being the key word. It's not going very well. I spend at least an hour on a language app every day and watch Dutch TV shows with subtitles. But my attempt to use Dutch in actual conversations has been futile so far. Whenever I try to buy coffee or something using Dutch, they blankly stare at me and say, "Can I help you?" in English.

When I'm not busy exploring the city and immersing myself in the culture, I help plan Sophie's wedding. Sophie was onto something. Being here is certainly helping take my mind off things. It's giving me the clarity I need. I'm even starting to see the silver lining in the events that I once thought had turned my life upside down. I'm thinking long and hard about my next career move. I've come to a realization that this might be the perfect time for a career change. I've lived all my life following a preset plan—college, grad school, a stable job, and marriage. Maybe it's time to shake things up or at least make a different plan.

As for Justin, being away from him is giving me a clear perspective on what wasn't working between us, other than the cheating, of course. I'm starting to realize that over the past four years, I was so entrenched in his world that I began to lose a part of myself. We shared everything—our apartment, lifestyle, and even friends. It didn't start that way intentionally. I always prided myself on being independent and being my own self. But as time passed, our lives morphed together until I no longer had my own separate life, except for my job. Maybe Justin's infidelity has saved me from making a colossal mistake by marrying him. As my mom would say, 'Everything happens for a reason, baby, even if you don't see it at the time.' Look at me turning into a glass-half-full kind of gal.

Some might say I'm avoiding processing my emotions by keeping myself occupied. But I'll leave that assessment for a therapy session I so desperately need. In any case, exploring new places and helping a friend by doing something I genuinely enjoy are the healthiest ways to avoid dealing with my feelings, if you ask me.

Exploring Amsterdam and wedding planning are not the only things keeping me occupied. Spending time with Daan—when we do wedding tasks together—, thinking about Daan, and fantasizing about Daan also take up a significant chunk of my time. I think about his piercing eyes, captivating smile, and well-built body more than I should. I think about other stuff too, stuff he could do to me or stuff we could do together. Saying he's living in my head rent-free is an understatement.

We also text sometimes after being forced to exchange numbers to coordinate our wedding planning tasks. Daan checks up on me even more than forgetful Sophie does. He texts me good morning every morning and asks how my day went every night. I have to admit his thoughtfulness is shattering my guards inch by inch.

I actually find myself missing his texts and looking at my phone in anticipation throughout the day. That's why I jump with excitement when my phone buzzes somewhere on the couch. It's Wednesday evening, and I'm sitting on the couch contemplating whether I should cook or order takeout.

What are you up to? The text reads.

Nothing. Just pep-talking myself into cooking. But we all know I'm gonna order takeout.

So you like homecooked food, but don't want to cook? He asks.

Thank you for succinctly putting my predicament. I respond, adding a winky-eye emoji to show my sarcasm.

Come to my place. I'm making dinner.

I debate internally whether I should accept the offer. I don't want to impose, but a homecooked meal sounds incredible right about now. Plus, deep down, I really want to see Daan. Who am I kidding? I know I can't say no to that.

Be there in ten minutes. I shoot the text and rush to the bedroom to change.

I jump out of the bathrobe I've been wearing since I took a shower two hours ago and change into a light brown sweatsuit.

Daan's place is not far from mine. I cover the fifteen-minute walking distance in ten minutes, driven by the prospect of a free meal and seeing Daan.

Daan engulfs me in a tight hug when I get there. I guess he's also happy to see me. The house smells like a delicious mix of spices, butter, and herbs.

"Ooh…what are you making?" I ask, perching myself on the kitchen stool.

"I made pasta with a creamy sauce and salmon. We also have veggies," he says.

Daan looks like he's in his element, chopping this, whisking that, stirring this, and tossing that. The whole scene is captivating, this extremely good-looking man having such an easy command of the kitchen. His arm muscles, exposed by his black t-shirt, flex when he's working. I don't know what looks more delicious—the food or the man making it.

"What?" he asks when he catches me ogling at him.

"Nothing. I'm just surprised that you can cook," I deflect.

"Why are you surprised?"

"Come on. Your family has a private chef. I can't imagine your parents teaching you how to cook," I say, leaning on the kitchen island.

He looks up from the pan, flashing that gorgeous smile of his. "You're not wrong. I picked up cooking when I was in the US. It turns out I enjoy cooking. I even took a few lessons."

"You took a cooking lesson?" I try to picture him in a chef's uniform, and my mental picture doesn't disappoint.

"Yeah, just for one summer."

"How can I help?" I ask, to make myself useful instead of simply drooling over Daan and the food.

"You can set the table," he responds.

I do as I'm told, and in just minutes, we're sitting with heaping plates of food. The food tastes even more delicious than it looks—buttery, creamy, and zingy goodness. I even let out a moan when I take my first bite. I notice Daan's face change with my reaction.

"This is amazing; you really are good," I say, going for another scoop.

He just stares at me, smiling. Is he staring at my lips, or am I imagining it? When our eyes meet, he breaks eye contact and stares down at his plate.

"What did you do today?" he asks, making a clear attempt to alleviate the tension.

"I took a ferry to Amsterdam Noord and walked around for hours," I respond, stabbing at my pasta.

"Nice. Tell me your favorite thing about Amsterdam," he asks, cutting his salmon.

"Oh, the canals, no question. It's nothing like anything I've seen in another city. I love the canals," I exclaim. I'm not exaggerating. I am in awe every time I walk by Amsterdam's canals, which are everywhere, that I have to stop to take in the view or take a picture.

After dinner, Daan asks me to stay for ice cream and a movie. How can I say no to that? But I don't tell him that I'm one of those people who easily fall asleep when watching a movie. As long as it's not a comedy or fast action, I treat every movie like a white noise machine, and I'll be in dreamland before it's even halfway through.

That was one of the things Justin couldn't stand about me. After trying for years to make me watch his favorite movies without falling asleep, he gave up. I even fell asleep in the cinema once. No matter how much caffeine I took before the movie began, I'd start dozing off after a few minutes, which drove Justin crazy. I honestly tried to focus, but I couldn't help it. I even used the 'I'm not asleep, I'm just resting my eyes' excuse a few times when Justin got mad. But we eventually decided not to watch movies together as a date night activity.

So I know I can't stand a chance when Daan picks a slow drama for us to watch. After I finish the ice cream, I feel my eyes getting heavy. The last thing I remember is resting my head on Daan's shoulder without even having a second thought.

When I wake up, my head is resting on a pillow, and a blanket is draped over me. I'm sleeping on Daan's couch. I look around, and he's nowhere to be seen. When I look at my smartwatch, I see it's a little after two in the morning. I'm too sleepy to even consider going home. I fall back to sleep.

In the morning, I wake up to the aroma of coffee wafting through the air. Squinting, still groggy from sleep, I glance toward the kitchen.

"How do you like your eggs?" Daan calls out. He's wearing a cream dress shirt with a tie. Even in my drowsy state, I can't help but notice how hot he looks.

"Scrambled," I groan, hauling myself from the couch.

I plop onto the stool, stealing another glance at Daan. "Why are you dressed up?"

"I'm pitching a new technology my team has been working on," he responds, carefully folding the eggs.

"Sorry, I fell asleep," I mutter, rubbing my eyes.

"No worries. I like having you around. I wanted to move you to the bed, but I didn't want to wake you. Hope the couch wasn't too uncomfortable."

He said he likes having me around. My heart flutters. He made me dinner, and now he's making me breakfast. Where does this man come from?

He places my scrambled eggs, buttered toast, and coffee in front of me. Then, he grabs his navy blue suit blazer and kisses my cheek as if this is a normal thing we do. "I have to run; you can stay as long as you want."

When he rushes out of the house, I'm left there, holding my cheek, which is still tingling from the touch of his lips.

Chapter Sixteen

The town of Lisse sits close to fifty kilometers southwest of Amsterdam. That's where Sophie's florist is based. The town is known for its beautiful tulip flower gardens that attract millions of tourists in spring. The famous Keukenhof Garden alone hosts over a million tourists for the few weeks it's open to the public.

Daan tells me that he has booked tickets for us to visit Keukenhof Garden before we have to meet with the florist. We leave Amsterdam early to beat the crowd and be there as soon as the door opens. The drive to Lisse is quiet. We sit in the car listening to music in comfortable silence for the most part. I don't feel the need to fill the silence as I usually do. The silence doesn't feel awkward either.

I stare out of the passenger side window at the beautiful countryside. It's amazing how you can just drive for a few minutes out of the bustling city center and see large farms and cows. Everything is in close proximity, which never ceases to amaze me as someone from the US.

We arrive at the Keukenhof Garden right when the gates open at eight in the morning. We're among the first people to enter the garden. Daan has thought this out quite well. He gives me what he calls "fun facts" about the garden as we walk around side by side, although I don't quite see the 'fun' part. He tells me that the garden extends over 35 hectares and has around seven million bulbs.

I'm blown away when I see the sea of flowers stretching as far as the eye can see. The flower arrangements and the greenery of the park are impeccably designed. I can honestly say that this is the most beautiful thing I've ever seen. A full sensory explosion in the best way possible: endless colors, patterns, and aroma.

Who knew there are this many types of tulips? There are hundreds of varieties of tulips in this garden alone. I now understand why Sophie has chosen to use them for her wedding; the possibilities are endless. In addition to tulips, the garden houses roses, lilies, and many others.

Daan takes a candid picture of me in the middle of the flower field, smiling from ear to ear in amazement.

"Look how pretty you look," he says, holding his phone toward me. With my colorful floral dress and my curly hair being swept by the wind, the picture looks magical.

We walk around the garden for a couple of hours. The place is getting crowded now. Exhausted, we take a break by the small pond surrounded by colorful flower arrangements.

"Wait here, I'll be back," Daan says, rushing to the gate before I have a chance to ask where he's going.

After a few minutes, he comes back, holding a picnic basket and a blanket. I can't believe he packed a picnic. How thoughtful. I look at him in amazement as he lays the picnic blanket and takes the sandwiches and drinks he brought out of the basket.

"Hope you're hungry." He sits on one side of the blanket and gestures for me to sit on the other.

"I'm starving. I didn't have breakfast in the morning," I say, sitting down and looking at the food with excitement. It seems like Daan has discovered the key to my heart: food. I grab the sandwich he hands me with enthusiasm.

"What is your favorite type of flower?" he asks, biting into his sandwich.

"Roses. I know, I'm a basic bitch," I mumble with my mouth full.

"Yeah, that's very basic. I thought you would be more adventurous than that," he says, laughing.

I glare at him with a fake pissed-off look. "I can say that about myself. You can't."

I also notice how good he looks in his black jeans and gray high-neck Henley sweater. When I see him taking a swig of the water and his Adam's apple bobbing, I have an intrusive thought of kissing his neck. I swallow, staring at his neck like a starving vampire.

"Why are you looking at me like that?" he asks.

I'm busted. "Um…nothing," I stutter.

We still have a couple of hours before our appointment with the florist. We decide to take advantage of this and bike through the tulip fields. We rent bikes and cycle around the tulip fields for the next hour or so. The tulips are planted in rows; each row is a different color, which gives the fields a rainbow effect. And I'm happy to report that I haven't fallen off my bike once during the hour-long bike ride.

In the afternoon, we meet the florist. She runs a family-owned flower farm and a floral shop. With her long golden wavy hair, long floral skirt, and a vest embroidered with flowers, she even looks like a flower. The flower arrangement options she shows us are all incredible.

Daan leaves the decision to me, as always. "I'm just your chauffeur and translator," he says when I probe him for his opinion. At some point, he even wanders off to God knows where when the florist and I start discussing the nitty-gritty details of flower arrangement and logistics.

Right when I'm finalizing the order, he comes up behind me and hands me a blush pink rose without saying a word. It's such a pretty flower, my favorite.

I'm fully caught off guard. "Thank you," I say, lifting the rose to my nose.

"You two are such a cute couple," the florist gushes, looking at us like one looks at adorable puppies.

"Thank you," Daan says before I open my mouth to correct her. I just look at him in amusement as he continues, "Who knows, we might come to you for flowers for our wedding too. But my lady over here prefers roses over tulips."

He puts his arm around my waist and tugs me closer. I just stand there grinning like a fool, holding the flower close to my fast-beating chest. What are you up to, Daan Peters?

"We have a wide selection of roses here. You'll even get a discount for using our services twice," the florist says, smiling at us.

She's a wonderful businesswoman. Who is going to tell her that we'll never be needing her services? At least, I won't be needing one. Daan might, but not with me. He might bring his actual future bride to this place to choose their flower arrangement. I find imagining him bringing another woman to this place, let alone marrying her, depressing.

"What was that about?" I ask when we leave the flower shop and head to the car. It's drizzling outside.

"Just acting out a fantasy," he says, opening the passenger door for me.

Right then, our phones shriek with an emergency alert. I jump, startled by the shrill sound. The text says that there will be a heavy storm in Noord-Holland until after midnight, and residents are advised to stay indoors.

Daan and I look up from our phones and at each other.

"We can't drive back today," he says.

"Would it be that bad?" I say with concern.

Daan keeps scrolling on his phone. "They are saying it's one of the heaviest storms the region has experienced in recent years. It can be dangerous to drive. We need to find a place to stay for the night."

"The town is swarmed with tourists. Do you think we can find a hotel last minute?" I ask. From what I've seen at the flower garden and tulip fields, thousands of tourists are swarming the small town. Even if half of them stay in town, I don't think the town has enough hotels to accommodate everyone.

"I'm not sure. I think I saw a hotel earlier just down the street. Let's start from there." He starts the car.

When we get to the hotel, the lobby is already crowded with so many people checking in. The hotel receptionist gives us an apologetic look before we even start asking if they have any rooms available. They don't.

Meanwhile, I'm on my phone trying to book something. Every hotel in the area is fully booked. I start to worry now. We can't even spend the night in the car when there is a storm. The heavy storm is mainly in North Holland, and we're in South Holland. But it's not as far away as one would think.

"Hey, it's gonna be okay," Daan says, looking at my worried face, and he squeezes my hand reassuringly.

We drive to the next closest hotel just in case they have a cancellation. But no luck. The receptionist says, "I'm sorry, everything is fully booked."

But right when we turn around and start walking out, he calls after us. We approach the reception desk with revived hope. "We just had a last-minute cancellation due to the storm. We have one room."

I sigh with relief. But I immediately get nervous at the prospect of spending the night with Daan alone, in the same room. What if there is only one bed? If there is one thing the rom-coms I've religiously watched taught me, it's the fact that there is always only one bed.

Chapter Seventeen

"Of course, there is only one bed," I mutter, more to myself than anyone else, when I step into the room. Daan is right behind me.

"Nope," he says, moving past me. "The beds are actually pushed together to create a king-size bed."

He pushes the beds apart without even breaking a sweat. And what do you know? There are two single beds. Whew… rom-com crisis averted.

The space between the two beds is not big by any means, as the room is also tiny. But it's definitely better than sleeping in the same bed and trying not to 'accidentally' touch each other. But if I'm being honest, what I'm afraid of is not being able to resist cuddling up to Daan and even doing other things. I don't need to complicate our relationship further. The boundary between us is shrinking as is.

"Dibs on the one on the left," I blurt out.

He releases that growling laugh that makes my heart skip a beat. "Is it because the one on the right is closer to the door?" he asks, giving me a knowing smile.

I throw myself on my chosen bed. "Maybe."

"We both know you're better qualified at fending off intruders," he smirks.

"You're not gonna let that go, right?" I say with an exasperated tone, covering my face with my hands. I don't want him to replay in his head the scene of me chasing him with a mop fully naked when we are stranded in the same room.

"Never."

I don't have a change of clothes. I think about what my plan of action is. I can't sleep with my outside clothes on. And I need to take a shower so bad. I wonder if Daan wants to shower too.

I open the closet, hoping to find a robe or something. As luck would have it, there is one. "There is only one robe. Do you mind if I use it?"

"Go for it," he says.

I retire to the bathroom to take a shower and change. I can't help but think about Daan in the other room when I'm naked. I try to imagine him naked. How his tall, lean body would look. How he would look in the shower with water running over his body. I brush off the thought and reprimand myself for being a creep. Instead, I let the hot water wash my sexual frustration away. Well, it only helps just a little bit.

When I return to the bedroom with my robe on, Daan is comfortably lying on his bed with one hand behind his head. He has taken off his sweater and shoes. Look at him, looking like a fitness model with his black t-shirt and jeans.

He smiles at me when I move past him and jump on my bed. The TV is on, and a rerun of some show I don't recognize is playing. Just then, I hear one of the male characters call a grown woman, "baby girl."

"Eww…that's such a turnoff," I groan.

"What?" Daan asks, startled by my sudden reaction.

"A man calling a woman 'baby girl'. Instant ick!" I exclaim in disgust.

Daan laughs. "Is that a common thing to say?"

"Not as common as it's in movies and books. But some people use it, and it disgusts me. It's one of my biggest pet peeves. If a guy calls me that on a date, I'll leave and never look back," I explain passionately.

"Noted," he smirks.

"What is yours? Your pet peeve?" I ask, curious to know what drives this calm and collected man unreasonably crazy, well, other than people calling the real football 'soccer'.

"'I don't want to…but' statements," he says.

I shoot him a confused look, tilting my head and raising my eyebrow.

"Like when people say, 'I don't want to be rude but…' and say something totally rude. Just say what you want to say. It makes it a hundred percent worse to preface it like that," he says passionately. "Also, when people say 'no offense' after saying something totally offensive. Either don't say it in the

153

first place or own what you say. Saying 'no offense' doesn't make it better."

"I love how you have strong opinions about things," I say, turning on my pillow to face him.

He chuckles, and we fall silent.

"I'll never call you baby girl," he says after a while. His voice is soft and quiet like it's coming from a distance.

"I don't want to be rude, but we'll never be in a position where you could call me that," I say, my cheeks burning for some reason. Do I want us to be in a position where he can whisper pet names in my ears?

He sits up on the edge of his bed, facing me. "Are you sure?" he asks with a daring look that makes me nervous.

I sit on the edge of my bed, mimicking him. We're facing each other now. The space between our beds is small for both of us, so our knees touch. But I don't move.

"I'm sure," I say, but my voice is so weak that it's not even convincing to me.

We stare into each other's eyes, daring the other person to break eye contact first. But the mood changes from confrontational to irresistible sexual tension. I have to resist my urge to jump on him and tell him to call me whatever he wants.

He leans in, resting his arms on his knees. I do the same. He's so close to me now that I can almost feel his warmth, which ironically sends shivers all over my body. I can feel my heartbeat quicken and my sensitive parts tingle. This man hasn't even touched me yet, but I'm already falling apart. I don't know if I can resist this, him, for any longer.

"Gemma," he calls my name softly, his voice not above a whisper. "If I kiss you right now, would you stop me?"

I should say 'yes.' But I don't want to.

"Why don't you find out?" I whisper back.

He leans in closer until our faces are only a few inches apart. I can feel his warm breath on my face. My lips part a little in anticipation. But he doesn't close the small distance.

His eyes scan my face until they land on my lips. His gaze lingers on my lips. "I need more reassurance than that, G."

"What kind of reassurance?" I breathe out the words than voice them. I can feel my lips quiver as the words leave my mouth.

"I need to know if you want me to kiss you, because I so badly want to," he says breathily, his voice coming off as tortured.

That breaks every little control left in me. "I want that too," I say.

His hand comes up to my chin, his thumb brushing the corner of my mouth.

He slowly leans closer until his lips brush against mine. I don't push him. He kisses me gently. I kiss him back. His lips are soft and firm at the same time.

He pulls away just a little and looks into my eyes. I can swear that I see his pupils dilate. We stare at each other for a moment we both realizing that things have changed between us. With the touch of our lips, we've crossed the boundary we've tried to maintain; at least, I've tried.

My lips tingle. I want more. I want him to kiss me deeper, harder. He cups my face and takes my lips in his hungrily, like he read my mind. A little muffled moan leaves my mouth, which is met by his deep groan. This time, the kiss is deep and passionate. I wrap my arms around his neck, pulling him closer. His tongue finds mine.

"I wanted to do this for a long time," he says breathily against my mouth.

"We only met two weeks ago," I smile, still kissing him.

"That's more than twenty thousand minutes," he says hoarsely.

I didn't know math could be sexy, but my insides ache when I hear that.

His hands move to my waist, and he hoists me onto his lap with one smooth movement. I'm now straddling him, feeling his firm body against mine. This feels amazing. We feel amazing together. Why didn't we do this earlier? Then, I remember why. All the reasons why Daan and I can't be together.

I abruptly stop kissing him and pull away just a little. "We need some ground rules," I say, panting.

He looks at me with confusion, trying to focus his hazy eyes. "Ground rules?"

"Yes. This can't be more than sex."

I see a disappointment wash over his face. It's subtle, but I notice.

"What if I want more?" he asks.

He's still holding me tightly, which makes it hard to stay reasonable. I almost say, 'fuck it, you can have more. You can have everything.' But that wouldn't be a rational thing to do, would it?

"I leave in two weeks, Daan. There is no 'more'," I say, gripping his neck for dear life. I'm worried that he doesn't want to do this anymore. I don't want to stop this. I'm too far gone, and I don't want things to go back to the way they were— where we don't kiss or touch each other. I hope this is enough for him.

"I'll take two weeks with you more than anything else. I'm in," he says, a smile flooding his face. His words not only warm my heart but set my inside on fire. A fire only he can put off.

I start kissing him again, running my fingers through his hair. I can feel his erection on top of his jeans. I grind against him to feel more of him, which makes him groan against my mouth.

He loosens my robe, and his hands travel under, eagerly exploring every curve of my body. He slides the robe off my shoulder, exposing my firm breasts that are displaying the effect he has on me. How bad I want him.

He gasps. "You're so beautiful, Gem."

He stands carrying me with him. My robe falls to the floor, leaving me fully naked except for my black thong. I wrap my legs around him. He gently lays me on my bed and settles on top of me, lifting himself up with one arm.

I take off his shirt with clear urgency. I want to feel his skin against mine. I gasp when my sensitive nipples press against his chest.

His hands travel to my core while his lips keep kissing me hard. Moving my thong to one side, he starts to gently rub all my sensitive areas. I release a loud moan against his mouth.

"What do you want?" he asks with a hoarse voice, his fingers still in my folds. What do I want? I rack my brain, but I'm too delirious to think clearly. I want everything. I want Daan. But even stringing words together is too difficult at this moment. Instead, I release a noise between a sigh and a whimper.

"Use your words, Gem. Tell me what you want me to do," he insists.

"I...I want you to make me come. I don't care how, just make me come," I moan than speak.

"That I can do." He smiles at me before he goes down. All the way down.

He takes off my thong, exposing my sleek core. I shiver in anticipation. He parts my folds with one sweep of his tongue. I whimper. When his tongue and mouth start working on my swollen nub, I moan louder than I probably should. This man knows what he's doing. It's like he has diligently studied my pleasure areas.

He drives me to the edge and stops to my absolute frustration. He comes up and starts kissing my neck, collarbones, jaw...everywhere except where he's supposed to. He's taking this slow despite my urgent need for release.

I try to guide him down, pushing his head. "Be patient; I want to take my time," he says kissing my neck. If only he knew that his deep, hoarse voice is making me even more impatient.

He goes down again. When his tongue and mouth resume their action, I arch my back, to feel more of him.

His right hand comes to my stomach, and he grips my thigh with his left arm, practically pinning me down. "Let me do the work," he groans.

So I let him. And boy, did he do the work. He sucks, licks, and strokes all the right parts until I'm all whimpering. I throw my head back and lock his head between my legs, my toes curling. He doesn't stop until I'm undone. Until my pleasure shoots out of me with my legs shaking.

He comes up and kisses me like I'm the best thing he has ever tasted. "Is it what you wanted?" he asks against my mouth.

I nod. I'm too weak to speak.

When I'm finally able to stabilize my breath, I push him to his back and settle on top of him, kissing his neck. That's when I fully register that he's wearing his jeans while I'm fully naked. I need to correct that.

I fumble with his jeans, and he helps me take them off. I notice with a gasp how his erection is protruding against his boxers. It looks big. I start kissing him on the mouth while rubbing his full length on top of his boxers. He's really big.

"Fuck," he growls against my mouth. I slide my hand under his waistband and start stroking. I feel him twitch on my touch.

"Your turn…what do you want? Tell me what you want, Daan," I whisper against his ear, almost nibbling at his earlobe.

"I want to be inside you. I want to fuck you until your insides contract around me. I want to make you come again while I'm inside you," he groans.

160

I like how this sweet, nice, and, at times, shy man turned into a demanding and possessive being who knows exactly what he's doing. Possessive in real life is a turnoff, but in bed, it can be a huge turn-on. I want him to do all the things he said to me.

"Let's hope you have a condom then," a graze my teeth on his jawline.

"I might have some in the car," he says.

I look into his eyes with surprise. "Did you know this is going to happen?"

"Did I know that there would be a storm and we'd be stuck together?" he says sarcastically.

I hear how unreasonable it sounds when he puts it like that. So, I rephrase my question. "No. Did you know we'd end up sleeping together?"

"I hoped. But I'm not that presumptuous. It was from some time ago. I'm not even sure if it's still there." He gives me one breathtaking kiss and flips me over. He lightly bites my lower lip until I forget what I was asking.

He then leaves me there and starts to put his jeans back on. But judging by the enormous bulge in his boxers, I don't think he can manage. Even if he does, he can't walk out of here with that.

"Give me the key, I'll get it," I say, getting up from the bed.

"No, it's cold and dark outside," he protests.

"I'll be fine. You can't walk out with that," I say looking at his compromising body part pointedly. He can poke somebody's eyes out with that thing, I think to myself, which makes me giggle internally. I almost say it out loud too. But I don't know how much humor is too much humor during an intimate moment. So, I decide to keep that to myself.

After considering my suggestion for a few seconds, he relents with a resigned sigh and hands me the car key.

I quickly put on his shirt, which comes close to my knees, and the bathrobe. Before I walk out of the room, I give Daan a long, lingering kiss to make him keep thinking about me until I return. The way he groans against my mouth tells me that he will.

It's not lost on me that I look ridiculous with my bathrobe and messy hair, but I rush to the car, short of fully running, with purpose and determination. I pray and hope that I find the condom in the car because I wouldn't hesitate to scour this entire hotel looking for one. That's how much I want Daan. As luck would have it, there's a packet. I sigh with relief.

When I return, holding up the condom in victory, Daan is standing in the middle of the room, waiting for me. He scoops me up and gently puts me on the bed, peeling back all the clothes I've put on.

I can't take my eyes off him when he stands up next to the bed, takes of his boxer, and slides the condom on his full length. It sets my insides on fire. I swallow hard.

He settles on top of me, parting my legs wide with his thighs. I feel him, all of him, against my opening.

"You're big," I say out loud without even thinking.

"I'll take it easy on you, sweetheart," he says with a hoarse voice, grazing my jawlines with his lips.

"No, don't," I say so fast. "I can take it."

Daan releases a chuckle mixed with a groan. "Say that again."

"I can take it," I say. "I want you…all of you."

"Good," he says and pushes into me. Slowly…one inch at a time.

"Oh Fuck, you're so tight…open up for me, baby," he groans.

I don't know if I can do that physiologically. But if this man asks me with that deep voice one more time, I'd open a bolted safe for him with my bare hands.

He grabs me by the waist with both hands, lifting me off the bed. He thrusts deeper…again and again, until his full length is inside me. I moan louder, gripping the sheets with my hands. I'm too close to the edge again. This feels better than anything I had before.

163

"I want you to come first…I can't hold for long. Come for me, baby," he instructs.

His plea is what has undone me. I call his name and mumble some inaudible things as I feel my insides contract against him as pleasure shoots out of me.

Not long after that, I feel him shudder against me. And he collapses on top of me. I hold him close and kiss the top of his head.

Chapter Eighteen

I wake up feeling the heaviness of Daan's arm on my belly. I can tell from the warmth and heaviness of his breathing on my neck that he's fully asleep. We're spooning—actually, more like pinned against each other in a single bed that's too small for both of us. My back is pressed against his broad, firm chest. My ass is perched between his lap. And there is something hard poking me. It's like his body automatically reacts to mine, even if he's asleep.

The events of last night keep replaying in my head. How Daan pleasured me in all possible ways. How demanding and insatiable he was. How his body shuddered on top of me when he was over the edge. How he gave me a long, gentle kiss afterward, like I'm the best thing that has ever happened to him. How he held me close like he'd never want to let me go.

For some reason, waking up next to him doesn't feel strange. It's like this is where we're supposed to be. What is strange is how safe and loved I feel when I'm around him. How close to him I feel in such a short time, like I've known him for a long time. Like we have so many shared experiences and memories.

I feel my guard coming down, which scares me, to be completely honest. I know I need to protect myself. I can't leave myself exposed to another heartbreak. So, I remind myself that this thing with Daan is just physical. We're just having fun. Nothing more. It can't be more, no matter how tempting it is.

I slowly turn around, wrap my arm around his waist, and rest one leg on top of his thigh. I hide my face in his neck, listening to his breathing. I just want to cuddle him and stay like this forever. My mind wouldn't mull over all the reasons I shouldn't be with him when I'm pressed against him like this, when our heartbeats match. We fit together so perfectly.

I feel Daan plant a kiss on the top of my head and pull me closer, if that's even possible. Lifting my head, I kiss him under his chin. I scoot up until our faces lie right next to each other.

Daan's eyes are still closed, but I can see a smile forming on his lips. I smooth his eyebrow with my fingers and kiss the tip of his nose.

"Hey, sleepyhead," I whisper.

"Hey," he looks at me, squinting.

"Exhausted after the night we had?"

His smile widens as though he remembers last night. He holds the back of my neck and pulls me for a kiss without saying a word. The kiss is slow, gentle, and passionate. It turns me into a puddle of warmth.

"Not exhausted enough to do it again and again," he murmurs, his voice still sounding sleepy.

"Good, because that's the energy I need for the next two weeks."

I think I see his eyes gloom a little. Is it a disappointment? You and me both, Daan. You and me both. Two weeks is not enough. But that's what we got.

I don't want to dwell on that. We've agreed that this is a two-week thing. "Now, let's get some food and head to Amsterdam," I say cheerfully. I'm starving after a night of panting and flipping around.

"Can we stay here just for a little longer?" he groans like a petulant child.

"Nope. You don't want to be around me when I'm hungry," I say, hauling myself out of bed and heading to the shower.

Right when I let the warm water run over my body, I hear the bathroom door open, and Daan walks in his full naked glory. He steps in the shower without saying a word.

I follow the water running over his firm chest, abs, and strong legs with my eyes. I then take a step toward him and trace the water over his body with my hand.

He puts a hand on my waist and pulls me closer, leaning in toward me. I stand on my toes and shorten the distance. We kiss until we can't breathe anymore, my hands gripping his neck. His arms are wrapped around me tightly until there is no space between us, even for air to fit in. He cups my ass and groans in my mouth.

"Last night was amazing...you were amazing," he whispers in my ear.

I feel his hardness against my stomach. When I grind against him, I feel it twitch and hear him loudly gasp. I like the effect I have on him.

He keeps softly whispering to me while kissing me. "You're gorgeous, Gem. Everything about you is gorgeous."

He's turning me into a puddle. I feel weak on my knees. If he were not holding me close with his strong arms, I'd crumble to the floor.

He traces kisses all over my face, mumbling compliments.

"I like how your eyes crinkle when you laugh." He kisses my eyelids.

"I like how your nose scrunches up when you're excited." He plants a soft kiss on the top of my nose.

"I like how your dimples dip when you smile; I'd pay a fortune to see that." He kisses both my cheeks, one after another.

"And your lips...oh, your lips drive me fucking insane, like I can't focus on anything else when I look at them," he groans before taking my lips for a long, lingering kiss. His tongue explores every corner of my mouth, until I fully melt against him.

Then, we relive last night all over again.

The devastating effect of the storm is evident when we drive to Amsterdam. Fallen trees and pieces of buildings are scattered on the sides of the road. It's a total contrast to the scenery we drove by yesterday.

Daan and I frequently glance at each other and smile like newlyweds during our drive. We even hold hands over the console. Daan takes our linked hands to his lips and kisses my knuckles, which flutters my heart.

When he pulls up in front of my apartment building, I'm not ready to say goodbye. I want to be around him for as long as possible. I can't believe I've gotten used to his presence this fast.

"Do you want to come in?" I ask sheepishly.

He puts his arm behind the passenger seat and leans in, giving me a questioning look. "Do you want me to come in?"

I can't help but notice how he consistently asks me about what I want. It feels like he's made it his mission to prioritize my wants and needs, which truly warms my heart.

I nod and peck his lips, but he doesn't let me pull away. He puts his hand behind my neck and pulls me into a lingering kiss. He doesn't have to say more. He wants to spend time with me as much as I want to spend time with him.

We spend the next several hours talking, cooking, and eating. Well, Daan cooks, and I walk around nibbling and tasting things. Why try to help when you have a chef with incredible skills? Plus, unlike Daan, I don't particularly enjoy cooking. It's something I do out of necessity. It's unsettling how he complements me in all perfect ways.

Daan tells me about his childhood, his time in the US, and his traveling adventures while cooking. He mentions that his mom used to take him with her during her business trips, and that's how he got the travel bug.

"So you're a momma's boy?" I ask jokingly.

He releases a weak laugh. "Used to be. But Mom and I don't see eye to eye on a lot of issues these days."

"Why?" I ask, popping a wedge of roasted potato he just took out of the oven into my mouth, which burns my tongue.

"She wanted me to work for the family business. She has this grand plan for Sophie and me to take over the company when she retires."

"So your mom wants you to take over a multimillion-dollar company. How terrible of her," I say, rolling my eyes.

"Okay, smartass," he tucks the curls that escaped my messy bun behind my ear. "I know how this sounds. It's a privileged problem to have. I have a lot of opportunities and privileges because of my parents' money. I can't deny that I had an easy life for the most part. But I wanted to do my own thing. Science has always been my thing, and I've never been into marketing and sales. Mom has a hard time accepting that we have completely different interests."

I feel bad for minimizing his predicament. I should know better than invalidating and dismissing someone's feelings and experiences just because they don't resemble mine. Daan and Sophie have everything I never had growing up—money, security, and two parents. But I might have something Daan didn't have: a mom who supports me no matter what. I can't minimize what not having that support feels like. So I give him an apologetic look, link our hands, and fiddle with his fingers, encouraging him to continue.

"Mom and I have a lot in common, personality-wise. We're both a bit uptight and control freaks, although she likes to use the term 'detail-oriented'. Sophie takes after Dad. They are carefree and spontaneous in a way that we couldn't comprehend. So, Mom and I had always been close when I was younger. We got each other until I refused to have anything to do with the family business and moved to the US. We slowly drifted apart after that."

"Sorry about that," I say sincerely. As someone who is very close to their mom, I'd be devastated if we drifted apart. My mom is my strongest support system. She's always been there, even when I mess up or disagree with her. I always know I can count on her.

"It's for the best. I don't mind how our relationship is now. Mom's attention can be suffocating, and I'm glad it's not directed at me anymore, to be honest," he says, pulling our linked arms to his lips. I'm not sure if he truly believes that. The subtle gloomy tint in his eyes is saying otherwise.

No matter how old or independent we are, it's natural to crave validation from our parents. It stings when they disapprove of our life choices, especially when that disapproval creates a wedge between us. It's disheartening when there is a condition to their love and acceptance. These are the people who are supposed to love us and accept us unconditionally. No matter what resources his parents poured into him and the privileges they gave him, that has got to hurt a lot.

I wrap my arms around his neck and look into his eyes. "It's her loss for not seeing how incredible you've turned out to be."

A faint smile spreads across his face, and he then kisses me like what I said means the world to him. This feels like another level of intimacy. It's strange how I feel closer to Daan with each passing hour. If we continue like this, we might achieve in the next two weeks what most couples do in two years, although we're not technically a couple. That scares me. The more I see Daan, truly see him, the more I like him.

We spend the next several hours talking and ignoring the show we've planned to watch. This is supposed to be a 'just sex' arrangement. But we spend more than ten hours without having sex in any shape or form. And surprisingly, I don't mind that one bit. As good as our physical connection has been, our emotional connection might even be better, which terrifies me. I don't know how I can be okay when this is over.

Chapter Nineteen

Helping Sophie with the wedding has reignited my passion for event planning. I've been putting off starting my own event planning business, waiting for the 'right time'. I don't want to do that anymore. There is never a right time. The universe has finally given me a fresh start, and I need to seize the opportunity. After years of contemplation, I've finally decided to take a leap of faith and start my event planning business.

I meticulously plan every aspect of my life anyway. I might as well make money off my compulsive need to plan and organize. The last four years I spent planning corporate events have taught me a lot that I can use for my business. Although corporate events are the last thing I want my new business to focus on, the knowledge and experience are transferable. Plus, I have been helping my friends and family members with their event planning for free. It's time to put my experiences to use.

I by no means think that this is going to be a smooth sailing. I'm not that delusional. Nothing in my life has come easy. I have to work hard and sacrifice a lot to get where I am. So, I know starting my own business from scratch is not going to be easy. But I'm finally ready to face whatever comes my way. I don't care if I have to live on my mom's couch until I'm back on my feet again. I'm no longer choosing the safe option—finding another job and securing a stable income. I'm taking chances for once in my life.

Driven by my newfound motivation, Monday morning, I wake up early to work on my business plan. I pile my curls on top of my head, put on comfortable clothing, and sit in front of my computer with a piping hot mug of coffee. I spend most of the day researching and drafting my business proposal.

I don't need much capital to start the business. I primarily need clients for now. It would be great if I can get an office space, but I know it's going to be super expensive in New York City. I look into co-working spaces and take note of the most affordable ones. I'll commence my search as soon as I arrive in New York.

Working with charts, Excel sheets, and a physical planner has dopamine coursing through my body. I haven't even realized that I skipped lunch until my stomach rumbles, waking me around five in the afternoon. Who am I to casually skip lunch? I usually don't fuck around when it comes to food. But the excitement and inspiration I feel today aren't giving me the time or energy to think about anything else.

Funnily enough, I don't even think about Daan. For the first time in such a long time, I feel a rush of inspiration about my future. Just by working on my business plan, I know more than ever that this is exactly what I'm supposed to do. I've found my calling, and it feels amazing.

Right as I stand up from my chair to stretch and search for food, a knock sounds on the door. When I open it, Daan is standing there holding a takeout paper bag. What a perfect timing.

I jump on him without thinking, which knocks the wind out of him, and he stumbles backward a little. But he catches me and carries me inside. He puts the bag on the dining table while still holding onto my clingy self.

"You missed me?" he says, cupping my exposed ass.

I'm only wearing an oversized t-shirt that cuts right above my knees and ankle socks. When I wrap my legs around him, my t-shirt bunches up and exposes my underwear that's barely covering my ass.

I run my fingers through his hair, looking into his gorgeous eyes. "Yeah, so fucking much."

He hides his face in the crook of my neck and releases a sheepish laugh. "What are you doing to me, G? I'm getting hard just for hugging you."

My breathing hitches by his tortured voice. If I was not deliriously hungry, I'd guide him to the bedroom skipping dinner.

"Good. That'll be my De-ssert," I say pointedly.

He releases his deep, growling laugh that rattles me to my core. I give him a long lingering kiss, slipping my tongue until I find his. A little preview of what's to come later. But first, food.

There's nothing more romantic than bringing someone food when they direly need it. You can't convince me otherwise. I'll fight anyone on that. I don't know about anyone else, but my heart is right next to my stomach. If you feed me, you're halfway to winning me over. Not that Daan needs that. He's already turning out to be one of my favorite people.

He's brought one of my favorite cuisines too—Indian. I take out the butter chicken, vegetable biryani, garlic naan, and samosas from the takeout bag, the delicious smell making my mouth water.

After we start eating, Daan asks, "Tell me about your business proposal," taking a sip of his water. I'd told him I was working on a business proposal when he texted me earlier, checking up on me like he often does.

"I'm planning to start an event planning business as soon as I get back to New York. I've wanted to do that for several years now. I think this is the perfect time for a career change. So, I've been trying to figure out capital, cost breakdown, office space, and funding opportunities. I'm very excited about it," I tell him, taking a bite of my samosa.

"Cool. How can I help?" he asks sincerely, with no hesitation, which warms my heart.

I smile at him to show my appreciation, although I can't accept his help. "Thank you. But I want to do this by myself."

Accepting help from Daan for my business would breach the boundary we're desperately trying to maintain. That would extend our arrangement beyond two weeks. But I don't tell him this part.

"I respect that. Just know that I care about you, and I'm here if you need anything," he says, not looking up from his plate, like divulging this information is leaving him exposed.

The words reverberate in my ears, "I care about you." I squeeze his hand resting on the table until he looks up at me. I wish he could see how much this means to me. Even if I'm not going to accept his help, the fact that he graciously offered means everything.

"Thank you," I simply say because I don't know what else to say. But I know that I deeply care about him too. If he needs anything, I'm here, even if I'm not ready to fully let him, or any man, in.

After sitting in comfortable silence for a few minutes, both of us preoccupied with the delicious meal, Daan asks, "Do you have plans for tomorrow evening?"

"No. Why?"

"I want to show you something. Be ready by five." He winks at me, as if there's a joke I'm not in on. He looks quite excited about the surprise too.

"What?" I ask. Needless to say that my curiosity is piqued by his attempt at being sneaky but failing miserably.

"It's a surprise," he says, grinning at me.

I bat my eyes adorably, well, I hope so, in an attempt to make him relent. "At least give me a clue."

"We'll be outside. So bring a jacket or something. That's the only clue you can get."

***

I'm excited and a little bit nervous about the surprise. I've tried convincing, and even tricking, Daan to tell me to no avail. As someone who likes to be in control, not knowing something in advance makes me anxious. However, I trust that Daan is perceptive enough not to take me to a place I won't enjoy.

When I look up the address he sent me, it's just a random street with no distinguishable features. I finally give up trying to figure out what the surprise is and brace myself.

When the time comes, I put on blue jeans, a black turtleneck sweater, and a gray trench coat with a waist cinch. I finish the look with my trusty ankle boots. I glance at myself in the mirror. I only have eyeliner, mascara, and lip gloss on. My sleek bun gives my face a chiseled look. I give myself a little pep talk. I'm ready for whatever comes my way.

Daan is standing with his hands in the pockets of his jeans when I arrive at the location. He looks as dreamy as ever in his signature black-on-black look: black jeans, a black overcoat, and black boots. The only pop of color is the blue-gray sweater he's wearing underneath his coat.

A smile floods his face when he sees me walking toward him. Something warm and tingly runs through my veins when our eyes meet, something that makes me nervous.

178

It's like locking eyes with an unrequited crush I've been pining over. It's been a long time since I've felt that way. What's happening to me?

"Hey," I say, trying to calm my nerves.

He pulls me into a tight hug, tucking my head under his chin. I melt against him. For some reason, his presence calms the tidal wave forming in my heart. I wonder how he has such an effect on me in such a short amount of time, how he makes me feel safe when my regular state is on edge.

He kisses my forehead and says, "Ready?"

I nod, my hands still gripping the back of his waist. "Where are we going?"

"You'll see, come on," he says, holding my hand and leading me forward. I follow without protesting.

When we arrive at Damrak Pier, "Ta-da," he cheerfully exclaims, pointing at a boat docked nearby. The skipper, wearing a captain's hat, waves at us.

"What's that?" I ask, awkwardly waving back.

"It's a boat," Daan says, purposefully playing dumb.

I nudge him on the shoulder. "I know. But why are we here?"

"You said the canals are your favorite thing about Amsterdam. So, I booked a private canal tour. Come on," he says, heading to the boat.

That's the most thoughtful thing any man has ever done for me. He listened to what I said and planned this whole thing, even though he didn't have to. He knows our arrangement doesn't require planning elaborate dates like this. He's just being good and thoughtful without expecting anything in return. I'm so touched that I have to swallow the tears that pricked my eyes. I'm trying so hard not to fall for this man, but he's making it extremely hard.

I follow him, and he helps me board the boat. I look around the small but beautiful boat with benches and a small table. That's when I notice the champagne, cheese and crackers, and a bouquet of roses.

"You did all this?" I say, looking at him with surprise.

"Jasper here helped," he says, gesturing to the skipper, who tips his hat in response.

"This is so sweet, Daan," I gush, kissing his cheek.

He turns a little red and breaks eye contact. I like how he gets shy sometimes. I feel like I make him nervous, and it kind of makes me happy. In these moments when we lock eyes, and he averts his gaze, I feel like he's trying to communicate something to me. Like he wants to tell me something, but he can't.

Seeing Amsterdam through its canals is a whole other experience. We cruise the city's waterways, marveling at the picturesque and historic architecture. The beautiful bridges and lush greenery we pass by leave me in awe. The sun slowly retires behind the buildings, painting the sky with a reddish-orange tint. The sunset bouncing off the water makes everything look magical. As dusk falls, we witness the city light up. The reflection of the buildings illuminated in the water creates another incredible scene. And experiencing this with Daan fills my heart with so much joy.

I snuggle close to him on the bench. He grabs a blanket and covers our legs, then puts his arm around me, pulling me close.

"Do you like it?" he asks quietly.

"More than you can imagine. Thank you," I say.

This night couldn't be any better. Even I, the self-proclaimed event planner, couldn't plan anything more romantic than this. It makes me wonder why Daan has planned this extravagant, romantic date when our arrangement is a two-week, just-sex extravaganza. I know, I know. It's not technically a date. But it feels like one. I can honestly say that this is the most romantic date I've ever been on, (if it were a date).

"Is this how you charm your dates?" I ask, looking up at him with a mischievous smile.

"Only the special ones," he responds and plants a soft kiss on my lips.

My heart jumps more than it probably should. I know he's just matching my banter. But I can't help but be extra delighted for being one of the special ones.

Chapter Twenty

Sophie and Lucas's new house is a quintessential beach house, with its sandy cream exterior and airy interior. The spacious two-story house is decorated with neutral, yet earthy, colors and a mix of modern and rustic furniture. The design choices and the way everything is arranged are immaculate, representing the personalities of both Sophie and Lucas. Sophie tells me that she used an interior designer when I compliment her design choices.

It's Thursday evening, and Sophie is having a surprise party—more like a small gathering of friends—for Lucas's birthday. Lucas is arriving late evening from his business trip to London. Sophie has invited his friends and some of her friends to the house. I arrive even earlier than everybody else to help her prepare for the party.

Sophie insists on having a tacos and margarita night. Apparently, Lucas really likes tacos, and she has to make them from scratch to show how much she cares. That's the response I get when I suggest having food delivered. So, I roll up my sleeves and get to cooking, following Sophie's lead.

A couple of hours later, Daan and Floris arrive, both just coming from work. My first instinct when I see Daan is to run to him and give him a long and deep kiss. But I resist my urge, knowing that we're not alone and Sophie and Floris don't know about our little arrangement. Instead, we give each other a restrained and a bit awkward hug.

Floris jumps at the opportunity when Sophie asks him if he can make the margarita. When I see his excitement, I know that he's going to make it extra strong, and I'm not mad about it.

"Gem, can you grab the can of beans for me from the pantry?" Sophie asks me at some point.

There is a large pantry adjoined to the kitchen. I scan the shelves filled with various food items to find the can of beans. Then I see it on the top shelf, just out of my reach. Standing on my toes, I stretch my hand as far as I can. I'm so close, yet I come up short. The shelves in this house are probably designed for Sophie and Lucas's height.

Just then, I hear the pantry door open, and Daan walks in.

"What are you doing here?" I ask, turning my head back to glare at him.

"I came to see if you need help. I know you're vertically challenged," he smirks.

"How dare you?"

Without saying another word, he comes up behind me and grabs the can with ease, proving that I'm indeed vertically challenged. He puts the can in my hand, but he doesn't move. Instead, he wraps his arm around my waist and presses against me. Gathering my hair to one side with his other hand, he kisses my neck. My breath hitches in my throat. The warmth of his breath, the firmness of his lips on my neck, and the pressure of his body pressed against my back are all too much.

"I missed you," he whispers, almost nibbling my earlobe. It has only been a day since we saw each other. We spent the night together on Tuesday after our canal tour, and we didn't get a chance to meet yesterday. But to be honest, I've missed him too.

Daan's mouth travels to the other side of my neck, planting soft, gentle kisses. I release a faint moan against my will. I need to stop this before we get carried away, although I really don't want to, if I'm being completely honest. But this is too dangerous.

"We have to stop. What if somebody walks in on us?" I say noncommittally.

He chuckles, his warm breath tickling the nape of my neck and sending shivers all over my body. "We tell them that we do this every so often."

I turn around to face him.

"That's not an option," I say, giving him a deep, lingering kiss that I know will make him hot and bothered. Before he reacts, I smile at him mischievously and rush out of the pantry with the can.

Luckily, Sophie and Floris are too caught up in their respective tasks of making tacos and margaritas to notice that we've been gone for a bit too long. Daan emerges from the pantry a moment later, shaking his head and winking at me when no one is looking. I've been feeling bad for not telling Sophie about this thing between Daan and me, but to be honest, this sneaking around feels good.

"By the way, Gem, I invited my friend Chris to meet you," Sophie says.

I glare at her in confusion. "Why meet me specifically?"

"You're both single. I feel like you two would hit it off," she says without looking up from what she's chopping.

I look at Daan instinctively. I see his face subtly change.

"You know I'm not really looking to date yet," I say, both to Sophie and to Daan, hopefully reassuringly to the latter. My decision not to tell Sophie about Daan and me might have backfired a little bit.

"Just meet him and see what happens. No pressure. I didn't tell him you would date him. He's such a nice guy. Plus, he's American too, and he lives in New York. He's just here to work on a project," Sophie tells me.

It seems a reasonable ask, just meeting a nice person with no expectations. "Alright," I say simply.

I look at Daan again, but he's not meeting my gaze. I want to smile at him reassuringly. If I'm not ready to date him, he better be sure that I'm not ready to date anyone else. I hope he doesn't take me saying "alright" the wrong way. I'm not agreeing to a date by any means.

185

"I didn't know you're playing Cupid, Soph. I've been single for three years, and you never offered to introduce me to any of your friends," Floris interjects, inadvertently breaking the tension I'm feeling.

"I don't have a friend I dislike that much," Sophie responds with a loud snort.

I burst out laughing, and look at Daan; he has a restrained smile. But when our eyes meet, he winks at me, which puts me at ease.

"Ouch. I'll have you know that I am a great boyfriend, and any friend of yours would be lucky to have me," Floris retorts.

"A great boyfriend who forgets about his girlfriend and leaves her behind," Daan chuckles.

"I didn't forget about her; It was an honest mistake," Floris responds with an exasperated tone.

Sophie and Daan are cracking up. But I'm confused.

"Somebody needs to tell me the story," I say, feeling left out.

"I was dating this girl for a few months, and we went to a concert in a big group, including these two assholes. We got separated at some point. I thought she'd gone ahead with Sophie and Julia, so I left without her. It turned out, she was in the bathroom and she stayed at the venue waiting for me after that," Floris tells me.

"You didn't call to check if she was with Sophie?" I ask, trying to stifle my laughter.

"No. In my defense, I was a bit drunk. I didn't even check my phone until the next day," he admits.

I can't help but laugh now. "What happened after that?"

"She broke up with me. That was the first text I saw when I checked my phone the next day," Floris says, earning chuckles from all of us.

"You guys are assholes," he exclaims, returning his attention to mixing the margarita.

After a while, we finish preparing everything we need, and the guests start to arrive. Sophie gives everyone a heads up that Lucas will be arriving in less than thirty minutes. All of us start speaking quietly, trying not to give away the party atmosphere in case he sneaks up on us.

When a couple of new guests arrive, I'm standing with Daan and Floris in the living room. Sophie opens the door and leads the two guys in our direction after giving them a quick hug. She introduces the guys as Chris and Andre. Oh, Chris.

"This is my friend I told you about," Sophie tells Chris pointedly when she introduces me to him. I wonder what she's told him about me.

"The famous Gemma, nice to meet you," Chris says, grinning from ear to ear. He has a nice smile, I notice.

"How famous?" I ask, smiling back.

"Sophie can't stop raving about her most gorgeous and intelligent friend," he says.

Chris is of average height and well-built. I can see his muscles stretching his formal-looking blazer. The man is handsome, I must admit. He also carries himself with the confidence of someone who has his whole life together.

"Sophie always oversells me," I mutter sheepishly. It's strange to have this conversation in front of Daan, especially when I see that Chris is liberally flirting with me.

"From what I'm seeing in front of me, she's very accurate with her description."

I don't know what to say to that. I just smile like a complete idiot.

"I mean, you're gorgeous," he adds, as if I didn't understand his not-so-subtle compliment the first time.

"Thank you," I say.

I steal a glance at Daan without making it obvious, but his expression is unreadable. He just stands there, sipping his drink. Floris, on the other hand, is chuckling, evidently following the flirtation happening in front of him. I feel so awkward in this moment.

Just then, Sophie saves me from this awkward situation by exclaiming, "Shush, everyone, Lucas is here."

We spend the next few hours wishing Lucas a happy birthday, eating cake and tacos, and drinking. Everyone is mingling and having fun, and I almost forget about the Chris-Daan debacle, the debacle I probably created in my own head. That's until Chris approaches me and asks to have a private chat.

We go to the kitchen, away from everyone. It turns out Chris is very easy to talk to; he's funny and extremely charming. I can see why Sophie introduced us. He tells me that he's a lawyer in New York and he's here to advise a multinational Dutch company his firm works with. He's clearly very successful and has his life together, as I initially assumed.

But I subtly try to friendzone him. If I had met Chris under different circumstances, I'd definitely go on a date with him, at least one date. But things are complicated right now. I can't even date Daan, the guy I'm hopelessly attracted to and genuinely compatible with, let alone go out with a guy I've just met.

But chatting with Chris is fun. It feels like having a piece of home. Talking to him about our shared experiences makes me realize how much I miss New York. We talk about the crazy things we've witnessed in New York and our experiences in Amsterdam. He tells me about the time his bike got stuck in tram tracks, causing a tram to stop, during his first visit to Amsterdam years ago.

I'm still laughing at that story when Daan comes into the kitchen. He looks startled when he sees us; I don't think he knew we were in here.

"Sorry, I just came to grab a beer," he says, heading to the fridge.

"No, you're good," I say.

Daan quickly grabs a beer from the fridge and leaves. For some reason, I can't shake this sense of guilt, even though I know I haven't done anything wrong. Daan and I aren't in a relationship. Even if we were, I'm just talking with Chris, and there's nothing wrong with that. But I have a sinking feeling in the pit of my stomach.

I keep chatting with Chris for a while, but I'm distracted now. I want to see Daan. We haven't had enough time alone this evening. When I excuse myself to rejoin the group, Chris asks me out directly.

"You seem like such a nice guy. But I just got out of a serious relationship. I'm not ready to date yet," I tell him.

"Fair enough. But can we exchange numbers? We can have coffee or something when we both get back to New York," he says. "As friends," he adds quickly.

"Sure." I give him my number and head to the living room.

I scan the room, looking for Daan, but I don't see him anywhere. I see Floris talking to someone I don't recognize, and I approach him.

"Have you seen Daan?" I ask, trying to sound as casual as possible.

"He left. He said he has work early tomorrow. You know how by the book that man is, and he gets cranky when he doesn't get his eight hours of sleep," he jokes, grinning.

I'm not in the mood to laugh at Floris's joke. But I plaster the fakest smile I can muster on my face, trying not to show my disappointment. All I can think about is how Daan left without saying goodbye, which bothers me more than I care to admit. I hang around for a while, not wanting to make my intentions too obvious. I need to see Daan.

I go up to Sophie and Lucas to announce that I'm leaving.

"I thought you were spending the night here. You can stay in the guest room," she offers.

I mumble something about having an early call and needing my laptop. I feel bad for lying to Sophie, but I can't tell her that I'm heading to her brother's apartment.

"I'll ask if Alexandra is driving to Amsterdam, and she can give you a ride," she says, referring to one of Lucas's coworkers who lives in Amsterdam.

"No," I protest. "I will catch the train."

I say my goodbyes and rush out. When I check my phone for the train schedule, I see a text from Daan. "Sorry I left without saying goodbye; I have an early call."

I reconsider my decision to go to Daan's place now. It's close to midnight, and he might want to go to bed early. But I can't resist this overwhelming need to see Daan. I decide to text him when I get there, and if he doesn't respond, that means he's asleep, and I'll leave.

"I'm in front of your building; buzz me in," I text him when I arrive at his place. I hope he isn't asleep.

I immediately hear the door buzz. When I arrive at his floor, Daan is already waiting by the door.

"Did I wake you?" I ask apologetically.

He doesn't respond. He just leans in and scoops me up by my thighs. This is more than the welcome I've hoped for. I wrap my arms around his neck and hide my face in the crook of his neck.

He seats me on the kitchen counter and steps between my legs. He hasn't said a word yet. He's just looking at me so intensely. He doesn't even break eye contact when I stare back at him.

"Why did you leave, Daan?" I ask softly.

He stays silent for a while as if reconsidering whether he should say what he really wants to say.

"I know I have no right to say this or even feel this way, but I didn't like it when I saw you hitting it off with that guy," he says, in a tone that tells me that it's hard for him to admit this. Daan was jealous, that's why he left. And why does that make me a little happy? Am I being toxic?

"I know you want to keep our relationship the way it is, and I respect that. I respect your decision, even if you want

192

to date someone else. I just...I just can't help how I feel, G. That's why I decided to remove myself from the situation. I'm sorry I left without saying goodbye," he adds.

My heart melts when I hear that. Just when I think this man can't get any better, he surprises me every day with his endless kindness and generosity of heart.

"We didn't hit it off. I mean, we got along, but not like that," I say.

"I understand why it makes sense for you to date him. You both live in New York, and he's apparently 'nice'," he says, imitating Sophie when he says 'nice.'

I chuckle. "If I'm ready to date, you'd be the first person I go out with," I say, grinning.

"Really?" he asks, a smile slowly spreading across his face.

I don't say anything else. Instead, I grab the back of his head and kiss him intensely, passionately, hoping that will tell him everything he needs to know.

Chapter Twenty-One

The rest of the week, Daan and I spend every night together, mostly at his place—talking, making love, Daan cooking for me, and me eating. We also go to the barn and ride horses. Well, Daan rides, and I cautiously mount the horse and hold on for dear life. I'm quickly getting the hang of it, though, thanks to Daan's patience in teaching me. I'm also happy to report that Miss Brenda is warming up to me. She no longer gives me side-eyes when I get close to her.

Most days, we talk until we fall asleep, waking up with our bodies intertwined. I can feel him pulling me close throughout the night when we drift apart. I also immediately close the gap if there is even an inch of space between us. I always want to be close to him. If I wake up before him, I stare at his sleeping face like a total creep.

Everything seems to come so easily with Daan. I often find myself opening up about things I don't usually share with most people. It feels natural and extraordinary at the same time, like nothing I've experienced before. Sometimes, it scares me how quickly I'm getting used to his presence. The time when I didn't know Daan feels so far away, although it was just a few weeks ago.

I'm getting used to us being together to the point that I find it hard to imagine not being with him. I feel a tug at my heart when I think about not being around him anymore. I try not to dwell on the fact that we only have one week left. But I can't help thinking about our looming deadline.

In addition to basking in Daan's captivating presence, I spend the week busy finalizing the preparations for the Peters v. Hofers sports tournament. The Peters have rented the whole sports club for the event. Teams representing the two families will compete in different sports. The women will compete in a football match—not what Americans call football, but the 'real football,' as Daan would say. I'm part of the football team representing the Peters' side.

The men, including Daan, are competing in a basketball match. "I thought football is your thing?" I ask when I first find that out.

"Yes, but apparently, having two football matches is boring," he responds, exasperated. It's clear that this is forced upon him by Sophie.

There will also be individual tennis matches, and the older people will compete in golf. Finally, the overall winner will be determined at the end of the day, followed by an afterparty.

It's going to be a whole-day event taking place on Saturday, a week before the wedding. The other two bridesmaids, Sima and Paige, our mutual friends from our grad school days in London, are coming for the event. They won't stay here for the whole week as they both have to work. They'll go back to London on Sunday and return next Friday for the wedding.

195

Early Saturday morning, Sophie and I head to Schiphol airport to pick up Sima and Paige. I'm so excited to see them. As we're waiting at the arrival terminal, we hear Sima's loud squeal before we even see them. She runs up to us and engulfs us in a three-way hug, shrieking about how happy she is to see us. In a typical Paige fashion, she stands back until Sima is done, and hugs each of us individually.

Sima is loud, outspoken, outgoing, and extremely extroverted. She could be whispering, but you can hear her voice from a mile away. When we first met, her personality was a bit overwhelming for me. But she won me over with her posh British accent and immeasurable kindness. She's a sweetheart. She puts up this hard-ass persona, but she's a softie at the core. Sima is also super smart, like extremely intelligent. After we finished our master's and most of us rejoined the job market, she pursued her Ph.D. And now, she's a lecturer at one of the top universities in the UK. She is certainly the full package.

Paige is the total opposite of Sima. She's a straight person to Sima's main character comedic persona. She's soft-spoken, introverted, and hates confrontation. Sima is always pulling her out of her comfort zone and putting her in uncomfortable situations. One would think she'd have gotten used to it by now. But no, she's perpetually mortified by Sima's shenanigans.

I haven't kept in touch with Paige as much since I left London. But Sima has remained one of my closest friends. Partly because of her consistent efforts to make sure we stay connected. I'm not naturally good at keeping in touch with people. So, I owe it to Sima and Sophie for being persistent and patient with me.

Sima and I sit in the backseat while Paige takes the passenger seat.

"How is teaching, Sim?" I ask as soon as Sophie settles onto the road.

"Exhausting. Remember how we used to complain about our teachers when we were students?" she asks.

I nod, recalling the days when we'd gather around, complaining about teaching methods, workload, and grades in university, mostly blaming our teachers for the whole ordeal.

"Nowadays, I complain about my students regularly. The entitlement some of my students have is truly astounding. Honestly, were we this self-absorbed when we were in their shoes? If I showed you some of the emails I receive from my students, you wouldn't believe it," she says with a heavy sigh. "They also make me feel so old. I don't know how the middle-aged faculty members are holding up. I find myself saying 'back in my days...' more than I care to admit."

We burst out laughing. At twenty-eight, Sima is one of the youngest lecturers in her faculty. If she can't relate to her students, I don't know who would.

"Well, I overheard an intern at my job describe the nineties as 'the olden days,' and I fell into an existential crisis," Paige interjects.

"It's all about perspective. I used to think being thirty is so old. But now that I'll be thirty in a few months, I feel younger than ever," Sophie adds.

"Forty is the new thirty now," Paige agrees.

We continue to complain about and look down on the younger generation for several minutes after that. It's funny how the older generation used to say all the mean things about millennials, and we used to get worked up about it. But now, we repeat the cycle without a second thought.

After a while, the conversation turns to the dreaded subject: Justin and my failed engagement. Sima and Paige express how sorry and disappointed they are about what Justin did.

"I want to see him when I come to New York. I just want to talk," Sima says pointedly.

She met Justin once when she visited me in New York. Like everyone else who knows him, she didn't see this coming. How could she? Even I, the person who spent almost every night with him in the past four years, didn't see that coming.

I squeeze her hand to show my appreciation for her unwavering support and willingness to fight my battles. "He's not worth your time."

"What did you do with the ring anyway?" Sima asks.

"I gave it back," I say matter-of-factly.

She cocks her head to the side a bit too dramatically and glares at me. "Why?"

I'm confused. Isn't that the norm? When you break off an engagement, you're expected to give back the ring, no?

"Because that's the right thing to do?" I say incredulously.

"Fuck that. You're not the reason why the engagement failed. He's the one who didn't keep his end of the bargain. If I were you, I'd sell the ring and buy myself something pretty. Or I'd party away all the money just to spite him," she says, wildly gesturing with her hands. Sima is not just loud with her voice, but she's also expressive in all possible ways. She's so captivatingly animated.

I cackle. "I see you haven't put the life of violence behind you."

Sima is always ready to fight. Most of the time, it's for a good reason. She doesn't start a fight, but she sure will finish it. She never backs down. Taking the high road is not in her vocabulary.

She used to get into a fight almost every time we went out in London, either defending herself or one of us. Although she cannot intimidate anyone physically, her fierce energy and words can be scary. Physically, she's even shorter than me. She's barely five feet tall with a tiny frame. But she wouldn't back down from fighting a man twice her size. In many instances, Sima, the petite superhero, had courageously faced giants to defend herself or her friends.

So it doesn't surprise me that she suggested selling the ring. That's a mild reaction in her book.

"I'll do that when men stop fucking around," she says through gritted teeth.

"So, never?" Paige chimes in.

Sima throws her hands in the air and exclaims, "Exactly."

"But these days, I'm cooped up in my office most of the time, and I don't have the opportunity to be violent. I actually have so much pent-up energy. This sports tournament better be good because I need to kick some ass," she adds.

Sima is representing the Peters in a tennis match as that's the only sport she willingly participates in. The rest of us are playing football.

***

The tournament kicks off with the football match. We're wearing black jerseys with golden stripes and writing, while the Hofers wear yellow jerseys with black writing. We hype ourselves up with ridiculous pep talks in the locker room before heading out to the field.

As the team captain, I stand in the middle of the circle the team has formed. "Ladies, the result of today's match will determine who will be dominant in Sophie and Lucas's marriage, both inside and outside the bedroom. So let's do this for Sophie," I say, moving aside and gesturing for everyone to link their hands in the center.

"Go Peters!" we scream in unison, unlinking our hands.

When we run onto the field, we pass by the Peters crowd. Daan stops me, tugging my arm gently, and whispers in my ear, "You look sexy in that jersey."

"I'll show you later how much sexier I can get out of it," I whisper back with a breathy voice. I laugh when I see the change of expression on his face. He looks like he wants to take me up on that right then and there.

As I turn around to join my team, I notice Julia squarely staring at us from the other side of the field. Her menacing expression sends chills all over my body. She looks like a fierce warrior in her jersey too.

The game starts slow, with both teams sizing each other up and playing it safe. But not even ten minutes into the game, Julia kicks the ball right at my stomach as hard as she could. The wind is knocked out of me, and I almost stop breathing. I double over in pain. When the pain subsides, I give her a 'what the fuck' look. She just shrugs unapologetically. Are we in high school?

"That's a bloody foul," I hear Sima scream from the bleachers.

When I look over, my eyes land on Daan, who looks like he wants to run onto the field. I smile reassuringly at him. I'm fine, and I'm going to get my revenge. Bring it on.

I initially thought this was a friendly match. Little did I know that Miss Julia is gunning for me. If she thinks her little stunt will hurt me and make me crumble in embarrassment, she has another thing coming. Cue hurricane Gemma.

She probably doesn't know that I played football in high school and college and was pretty good at it. I can single-handedly take on Julia and her minions. Most of them are tall, so not technically minions. But you get the point.

The moment my teammate passes me the ball, I forge ahead, dribbling past the opposing team's midfielders and defenders, who try to stop me unsuccessfully. I'm fast and agile. The crowd is cheering for me, Sima's voice the loudest among everyone.

The last person standing between me and the goalkeeper is none other than Julia. I lock eyes with her, flashing a villainous smile before passing the ball between her legs and meeting it on the other side before she even registers what's happening. *You got nutmegged, Julia.* Sorry, Michelle Obama, but sometimes when they go low, I go lower. I can be petty as hell. The goalkeeper doesn't stand a chance. I score the first goal for my team.

I run to the side where the Peters are cheering and slide on my knees. I might have scraped my knees, but it's worth it. I glance at Daan and see a mix of pride and surprise in his eyes.

I bet he didn't know I'm this good with balls. Well, with this type of ball.

No one can stop me after that. Many of them even quit trying. They get tired before even the first half is over, and they helplessly watch me pass left and right. I have a free rein in that field. Julia's stunt makes my competitive side come out, which takes me back to my college days when I used to give it all— 'leave everything on the field,' as they say—whenever we competed against other college teams.

I score the second goal with ease. Sophie and I chest bump in celebration. Bad idea. We both grab our boobs in pain. The Hofers manage to score one goal when our defenders are distracted. For the third goal, instead of scoring it myself, I pass it to Sophie so that she can have her moment. She doesn't disappoint. She sticks it.

But I'm not done. I'm going for a hat-trick, and no one can get in my way. So I don't stop, even though it's clear that we've secured a win. Just a minute before the referee blows the whistle, I score my third goal, the fourth for the team. When I run to our side, Daan runs up to me, lifts me and spins me around with delight. Julia must be raging. But this time, I don't care.

Chapter Twenty-Two

I'm celebrating our win and basking in the admiration of the Peters when Daan leans close to my ear and whispers, "Follow me to where the locker rooms are." And he walks away without waiting for my response. It takes me a while to register what he just said or implied.

I awkwardly hang around for a few minutes, trying not to blow our cover before I head the way he disappeared. No one knows that Daan and I are doing what we're doing. Not even Sophie. Normally, I tell Sophie everything, but I feel weird about telling her that I'm sleeping with her brother. She probably wouldn't care, but it still feels strange to me for some reason.

When I enter the building and turn toward the locker rooms, Daan is nowhere to be found. I look around in confusion. The long hallway is cold and empty. I don't know if he's waiting for me in the men's locker room. I know he wouldn't dare to enter the women's locker room. I just stand in the corridor, not knowing where to go. I'm not gonna enter the men's locker room and risk seeing someone's flaccid dick or, even worse, butt crack.

"Daan," I call out hesitantly, my voice still low, trying not to attract attention. It still echoes ominously.

All of a sudden, a door opens and a hand pulls me inside before I realize what's happening. Daan locks the door behind me and pins me against it, his mouth hungrily taking mine. I'm caught off guard, breathless. But I like the pressure of his body against mine. I run my fingers through his hair and pull him closer.

When we pull away just for a second, I notice that we are in a cleaning supply closet. It's a tiny room, another reason to stay pressed against each other. Turning me around, he pushes me to the table, holding a stack of paper towels. He knocks the paper towels to the floor and lifts me onto the table in one smooth movement. The hungry, demanding Daan is here, and I'm enjoying every minute of it.

Daan's mouth travels to my neck, his kiss sending shivers all over my body. "I'm all sweaty," I say breathily, feeling a little self-conscious.

"I don't care," he says, his mouth still on my neck.

His hungry kiss leaves me wanting more—more of him. I wrap my legs around his waist, forcing him to get closer until I feel his erection against my core. I let out a sound somewhere between a gasp and a moan.

Daan pulls back just a little and pulls down both my shorts and underwear in one smooth motion. I see him produce a condom from somewhere. I gasp in anticipation. He puts the condom between his teeth and pulls down his shorts just enough to expose his raging member. He quickly wraps himself up and pushes against my opening.

"You looked so damn hot in that field. Where did you learn to play like that?" he says, pushing into me, inch by inch.

"High school…college," I breathe out the words. I'm too breathless to speak in full sentences.

I cling to his neck as he pushes deeper and deeper into me. Again and again. He groans loudly, and I feel him pulse inside me. He's undone, hiding his face in my neck and breathing heavily. But I'm not there yet. He doesn't pull out. He stays inside me and slides his hand between us. The fullness of him inside me and the pressure of his fingers on all my sensitive areas drive me over the edge.

After we're done, he holds me close and rests his forehead against mine. We stay there for a while like we're both afraid to let go. This feels like an extra level of intimacy. What's this man doing to me? He shatters every ounce of control I desperately try to maintain.

***

Not long after, I'm sitting next to Sima, watching the basketball match. Daan might be good at football, but he's a terrible basketball player. So are all the men on the field, except a couple from the Hofer's side. Looking at how tall most of these men are, one would think they'd be decent at handling a basketball. But no, all this height is wasted for nothing.

The consolation for watching this terrible game is staring at Daan for close to fifty minutes without anyone thinking that I'm an unhinged creep. He looks so good in his basketball jersey that accentuates his tall, firm frame. His basketball skills, or lack thereof, don't deter me from shamelessly thirsting over him. My eyes are following Daan instead of the ball. I can't tell the score if anyone asks me.

My mind went to what we did just thirty minutes ago. How he hungrily kissed me. How his body was pressed against me. How he felt inside me. How he held me afterward like this means more than what it is.

I'm lost in my own thoughts until I notice Sima staring at me. "What?" I ask.

She looks at me, then at Daan, and then back at me pointedly. "What's going on between you two?"

I don't answer, but I feel the heat on my face. I don't mind telling Sima about Daan and me, but this is neither the place nor the time. We are literally surrounded by his family members and friends.

"Oh my God, you're sleeping together," she exclaims, wide-eyed.

I know nothing would escape that brilliant brain of hers. She looks at me once and reads all my secrets.

"Shush, stop screaming," I say, glancing in Sophie's direction. She's sitting two rows in front of us with her parents and Paige. "Nobody knows."

"So you're sleeping together?" she asks in a quieter voice. Well, quieter for her.

I nod, hoping this will stop her insistent questioning. But if I know Sima, she's just getting started.

"So, are you dating? I need more details," she says, her voice rising slightly at the end.

"No. We're just…it's just sex," I whisper.

"Okay… how did this come about?"

"You know I'm helping Sophie with her wedding? She sort of teamed Daan and me up to take care of wedding stuff. We got closer and became friends," I explain in a hushed tone.

Sima looks at me with a raised eyebrow. "So you're friends with benefits?"

"I guess you could say that," I shrug.

"So it's no strings attached?" she asks again.

"Yes," I answer with an exasperated tone.

"You know where I'm going, right?" she asks pointedly.

Then it hits me. "I know what you're going to say. I've watched both movies."

"If you did, you know that this is a bad idea. There is always a string attached. One person always falls in love," she says.

"But this is different," I retort defensively.

Sima raises her hands in the air, shaking her head. "How?"

208

"First of all, this is real life, not a movie. And Daan and I have legitimate reasons for why we shouldn't date," I try to explain with a reasonable tone, which is hard to do when you're whispering. Is it only in my head that this makes sense?

"What reasons?" she asks, raising her eyebrows.

Sima's confusion surprises me because she's often the first person to say that long-distance relationships are impractical. That's exactly what she said when I tried to set her up with my friend, Coby, when she visited New York. She was staying in New York for a few weeks for her research fellowship at Columbia University, and Coby often traveled to Europe for work. So, I thought they could make it work. But a long-distance relationship was not even worth the try, according to her. So why is she now not getting that at least Daan and I have that as a valid reason for not being together more than physically?

"For starters, we live on the opposite sides of the Atlantic. And I'm not ready to seriously date another person after what happened with Justin." I pause, hesitant to mention the third reason. "Plus, Daan still has feelings for Julia," I add a bit more begrudgingly than I intended.

Sima gives me a puzzled look, her brows knitted together. "Julia?"

"Yes. They used to date, like seriously date. He almost proposed to her before she broke up with him." It stings to think about Daan and Julia. Not just because she's not my favorite person at the moment, but also because I don't like the idea of Daan being in love with another woman. I know it's irrational, but I can't help it.

"But you look nothing like her," Sima blurts out.

"Geez, thanks," I say, rolling my eyes.

"I didn't mean it in a bad way. Nobody can deny that you're gorgeous. It's just that the man doesn't seem to have a type," she clarifies, nudging me on the shoulder.

I smile at her for calling me 'gorgeous.'

"Did he tell you he still likes her?" she asks.

I know Sima won't let this go until I tell her every single detail. I'm partly grateful because I've been keeping this thing with Daan to myself, and I desperately need to share it with a friend. And Sima is the perfect person for that.

"No. Sophie kind of implied, and I assumed."

Sima gives me the 'why do you assume when you can ask him' look. She's not wrong. I could ask Daan about how he feels about Julia. But I feel like I don't have the right to do that. I can't date him either way, and there is no reason for me to probe him about his feelings about someone else. I'm the one who boxed us into the 'no strings attached' territory. He literally doesn't owe me anything.

"I'll tell you more later when we are not surrounded by other people," I whisper to her.

I don't want to talk about Daan and me any more right now. I'm not ready to rethink the reality of what I've gotten myself into. Instead, I divert my attention to the game and watch the Peters lose miserably.

Sima is not wrong, though. This 'no strings attached' arrangement might not end well. I'm afraid that I'll be the one who ends up catching feelings and risking heartbreak.

Chapter Twenty-Three

Overall, the Peters win the sports tournament in a landslide. Basketball is the only match the Hofers manage to win. Needless to say, we set Sophie up for success in the marriage she's about to embark on. Now she can always throw at Lucas's face that his family and friends suck at sports whenever they get into a fight. After all, if marriage is not about keeping score and staying ahead, I don't know what it's about.

I make sure to point that out in front of Lucas too, and he takes it with his chin held high. Surprisingly, he's not as devastated as someone who just got his ass handed to him. One would think he'd be too embarrassed to show his face in public from the way his family and friends sucked at almost every sport. But no, Lucas doesn't seem to care one bit.

After the tournament ends, the afterparty follows in a huge venue with an open bar. With cocktails and shots flowing left and right, almost everyone is trashed after the first hour. I mingle with both the Peters and Hofers crowd and enjoy the fifteen minutes of fame I deservedly obtained because of my football skills. I chug beers with cousins of Lucas who are in college; I gossip about the social elites I know nothing about with the rich relatives of Sophie; and I play pool with Lucas's middle-aged uncles, who I caught drunkenly glancing at my backside a couple of times. Before the glancing turns to groping or I catch a hand from their wives, I excuse myself and go to the bar.

This is to say that I'm having the time of my life. This is the most fun I've had in a long time. I didn't even need or rely on Daan to have fun. Don't get me wrong, Daan has greatly contributed to my joy throughout the day. But I also have so much fun without him, with strangers I haven't met before and in a culture I'm not fully familiar with. Daan gives me my space too. When our eyes occasionally meet across the room, he smiles or winks at me reassuringly. I know he's there if I need him, but I can mingle and charm my way through the party on my own.

This feels so much different from my codependent relationship with Justin. Not that Daan and I are in a relationship. But if we were, I know it'd be so much different from my previous relationship. I'd not lose my individuality and independence this time around. Who knew this chaotic and fun day could render itself to self-reflection? It's through the little things that we learn the biggest lessons.

Just when the bartender hands me my drink, a mojito, Floris approaches me with his usual boyish grin. He looks extra cheerful today, which I suspect has a lot to do with his level of drunkenness. It doesn't take a genius to tell that he's already drunk, but he orders another drink without any hesitation.

From the few times I've met him, I gather he goes all out. I've heard him loudly announce, "You know me, I work hard and play hard," a few times whenever someone suggests taking it easy. He doesn't have the natural restraint of Daan and Lucas. I can tell he's the one pushing them to do wilder things while they try to keep him level-headed. I guess the balance works well for them.

"Gemma, remind me to nominate you for the next Ballon d'Or," he says, referring to the biggest football award in the world. He's slurring his words just so slightly.

"I'm flattered," I say, taking a sip of my mojito. The bartender didn't skimp on the rum. When I look over at him, he winks at me. I mouth 'thank you' to him.

"Honestly, you were really good…like pro-level good," he adds.

"Well, I don't know about that. I was playing with people way less experienced than me," I say humbly.

After a while, Floris shoots me a questioning look, though I don't understand what it's about. Then, a mischievous grin spreads across his face. "What are you doing to my friend, Gemma?"

"Daan?... What do you mean?" I ask, confused.

"Who else… don't think I didn't see you two getting extra cozy. And he won't shut up talking about you," he says. "When I ask him what's going on between you two, he just says 'nothing.' But it doesn't look like nothing. Even today, he's been following you with his eyes while you're obliviously walking around the place."

His natural forwardness and the alcohol are a dangerous combination. Floris basically has no filter at the moment. He's spilling all the tea. So, I can't help taking advantage of the moment, and probing a little bit. I don't even pretend to deny that I'm nosy.

"He talks about me when I'm not around?" I ask, blushing a little.

"All the time. It's all Gemma said this, Gemma did that, and I did this and that with Gemma… he won't shut up," he says with an irritated tone.

Daan talking about me when I'm not around without even telling his friends that we're sleeping together flutters my heart. He must think about me when I'm not around too. And for some reason, knowing this stirs butterflies in my stomach. Oh boy, I'm in deep trouble.

"Even now, look at him looking at us," Floris points to Daan, who is standing on the other side of the venue with a couple of older people I don't recognize. Floris isn't wrong; Daan is looking directly at us, or rather, just at me. When our eyes meet, he quickly averts his gaze, and a smile floods my face.

Floris alternates his gaze between Daan and me pointedly and says, "Whatever is going on between you two, it's cute. I approve."

I laugh without confirming or denying anything.

Floris leaves, loudly announcing his urgent need to use the restroom, and I stand there alone, considering which small group to join next. Maybe I'll grab Daan and stare at him until he shyly averts his gaze as he often does.

As I'm about to leave to do just that, Julia approaches me, sipping her drink through a straw. Talk about throwing cold water on my excitement. I don't know what she wants. Maybe she wants to apologize for kicking the ball right into me unprovoked?

"I didn't know you're such a good football player," she says with a hint of bitterness in her tone.

"Yeah, I played in high school and college," I reply briefly.

She doesn't bring up the game again. Rather, she asks me out of the blue, "When are you going back to New York?" Her tone doesn't display curiosity. Instead, it kind of says, 'please go back to whatever hole you crawled out of.'

I choose to give her the benefit of the doubt and answer her question. "The day after the wedding."

She scoffs. She actually scoffs in my face.

"Honestly, Julia, I don't know what your problem is. You've been rude to me since the day we met," I say, feeling annoyed. I don't know if this is her true personality or if she simply dislikes me for some reason.

At this point, I'm done with her. I don't want to be part of whatever game she's playing. I don't care if this is related to Daan or not. They can deal with whatever lingering feelings are left between them on their own. But respectfully, I need Julia to leave me alone.

Instead of responding to what I said, she asks, "Why did you lie to me?"

"About what?" I'm flabbergasted. I haven't had enough interactions with her to even have a reason or opportunity to lie.

"You told me you and Daan are just helping Sophie with the wedding coordination, and nothing is going on between the two of you," she says, appearing proud of her gotcha moment.

"That was the truth, at least at the time," I reply curtly. I don't feel the need to explain what's happening between Daan and me. I don't owe her anything, to be honest. If she wants to know, she can ask Daan.

"There's clearly something going on between you two. I saw you sneaking out of the supply closet earlier, looking all disheveled," she says with a look of disgust on her face.

I don't deny it or attempt to explain. With all due respect, that's none of Julia's business.

"Why do you care anyway? You're the one who broke up with him. Do you still have feelings for him?" I ask, my tone exasperated.

I'm annoyed. I don't want to engage in this confrontation. Fighting over a man is the last thing I want to do. I've never done that before, not even when I was a teenager, and I won't start now. This whole thing sounds so immature.

217

"I don't have feelings for Daan. But I still care about him. He's my friend. I don't want him to get hurt by someone who is using him as a holiday pastime," she retorts, looking me dead in the eyes.

I'm exhausted at this point. I'm this close to walking away from this conversation. "I'm not using him as a holiday pastime. You don't know anything about what's going on between us."

"Whatever is going on between you, will it continue when you go back to New York?" she asks.

I don't answer her, but the expression on my face says everything. What's happening between Daan and me has an expiration date. It'll be over in a week when I return to New York.

"That's what I thought," Julia says smugly, walking away without waiting for my response.

I want to be mad at Julia. I am mad at Julia. But I can't get rid of this nagging feeling that she might be right. After this is over, one of us, or maybe both of us, might end up getting hurt. From the way my heart leaps whenever I see Daan and the way I constantly think about him when he's not even around me, I'm afraid the one getting hurt might be me. I'm even more scared that I might end up hurting him. I know what heartbreak feels like, and Daan doesn't deserve that.

But there is no point in dwelling on this now. I've made my bed, and I gotta lie in it. I need a fucking drink. When I'm heading to the bar, I'm stopped by Sima and Floris, who call my name loudly—even louder than the loud music—and wave wildly, gesturing for me to come over. They're sitting around a table at the corner of the venue. It looks like they are engaged in some sort of drinking game. Perfect; that's exactly what I need.

I join the 'never have I ever' game they're playing to get to know each other. The problem is, at this point, the game has turned into mentioning ordinary things that everyone has done at some point. Like "never have I ever peed a little when I was laughing hard"; "never have I ever talked shit about my boss"; "never have I ever snuck contraband into the movies"; "never have I ever fallen off a bike." (The last one is clearly my prompt). So, it doesn't take long before we're extremely drunk—slurring words, stumbling to walk drunk. I don't know how Sima and Floris manage to do this, but they keep playing the nonsensical game and drinking, while I leave to go look for Daan.

I scan the venue, looking for a handsome, tall, and blonde man. I don't know if the alcohol is clouding my vision, but I don't see Daan anywhere. I give up on looking for him and stumble outside to get some air.

Then I see Daan standing on the balcony, leaning on the railing. I wrap my arms around his waist from behind and hide my face on his back.

He turns around to me and lets me lean on his chest. "Hey," he says softly.

"Why are you so cute?" I slur, looking at his face hazily with my chin planted on his chest.

"Why are you so cute?" he repeats my question.

I pull away a little, ready to argue my case that he's cuter than me by all standards. This is a hill I'm willing to die on. "You're this cute; I'm only this cute," I say, demonstrating our respective levels of cuteness with my hand movements.

Daan laughs. That deep, growling laugh. Even in my drunken brain, I'm so happy that I made him laugh. Daan's laugh is such a pure expression of joy that I don't even mind embarrassing myself to make him laugh. Maybe I should ask him to record himself laughing for me to take to New York, I think to myself.

"What would you do with a recording of me laughing?" he asks, chuckling. Oops, I guess I said it out loud.

"I'll listen to it when I feel sad or lonely," I respond, playing with his shirt collar.

"You can always call me when you feel sad or lonely," he says, looking deeply into my eyes. I know he's serious because he doesn't smile when he says that. That both warms and breaks my heart a little.

"But that will defeat the whole purpose of our arrangement," I say.

He cups my face gently. "I know, but just know that the offer is always on the table."

I remain quiet for a while, thinking about what he just said. I imagine myself calling Daan when I feel lonely or sad and hearing his deep voice through the phone. I imagine us talking at night until we fall asleep.

"You're totally a husband material. I'll let you put a baby in my belly," I say, protruding and rubbing my stomach.

Daan laughs even louder and says, "You're adorable when you're drunk."

"I'm not drunk," I say defensively, crossing my hands over my chest.

"Okay. Can I get you some water or something?" he says, pulling my arms apart.

"You still think I'm drunk. I'll prove it. Test me," I challenge him with a defiant look on my face.

"No."

"Test me."

"Alright," he relents. "Walk in a straight line."

"Easy," I say, walking in a straight line and stretching my hands out to balance myself. I look like I'm trying to walk on an imaginary rope. Despite my best efforts, I stumble like an absolute idiot.

Daan shakes his head in amusement.

"It's not fair. I'm wearing heels," I whine.

I see him trying to stifle a laugh. "Okay, say the alphabet backwards."

"I can't even do that when I'm sober."

"So you admit that you're drunk," he says, pulling me close. He pecks my lips. "You're so adorable."

"Why do you have to be so charming, hot, and considerate?" I say with a whiny voice, as if those are undesirable qualities. Truly though, it's not fair that he's all this and more. Especially when I know that I can't date him; that he can't be mine. How could I stop myself from comparing every man I meet moving forward to Daan? The bar is set high now, and only Daan can reach it, literally and figuratively.

"Why not?" he asks between short kisses.

"Because you make it so easy to fall in love with you. I don't know how I'll cope when you're not around anymore," I say, feeling tears prickle my eyes. I plead with my drunken brain not to make me cry.

The expression on his face changes, but I'm too drunk to read it. "How much did you drink, G?"

"Just the perfect amount. You don't love me?" I ask. I really am drunk. What the heck am I saying?

"Of course, I love you," he laughs. I know he's just entertaining my drunken foolishness. But there's something in his tone I can't quite place. Is it yearning? Sincerity? I wish I had my full cognitive abilities to discern that right now.

"No. You love Julia. You don't love me," I whine like a petulant child.

"What? That's not true," he says. But he's still laughing. Laughing at me. I feel like crying.

"Why are you crying?" he asks. I must have been crying for real.

"Because I'm unlucky in love."

Daan takes me inside and feeds me some pastries, which I don't know where he got them from, and almost forces me to drink so much water before driving me home. I don't speak much on the drive. I'm drifting in and out of sleep the whole way through. One time, I doze off and wake up with a burning question.

"Would you still love me if I was a worm?" I mumble without opening my eyes.

I hear Daan laugh before he says, "Yes, I would."

I can sleep in peace now.

Daan carries me up to my apartment, although I'm a grown adult who is fully capable of walking. But I don't protest. I just happily allow him to carry me. After he puts me in bed, I feel him take off my shoes and clothes and slip an oversized t-shirt on me before tucking me in bed. The last thing I remember is asking Daan not to leave me alone.

When I wake up with a stinging headache a few hours later, he's still here, sound asleep next to me. I slowly sit up on the bed, trying not to move my head. That's when I see the bottle of water and painkillers on the bedside table. I know this is Daan's doing. How thoughtful of him. I take two pills and down the water, and I lie back down on the pillow, looking at Daan.

That's when the events of the night before start replaying in my head. The thing about being drunk is unless you're fully blackout, you'll likely remember everything you did and be mortified the next morning. All the embarrassing details. The memory could be foggy, but you'll still remember.

So the memories from the night come flooding, piece by piece. Did I really ask Daan to put a baby in my belly? What is wrong with me? I told him I loved him, and I forced him to say he loved me too. I know that was not serious, and he was just joking and entertaining my drunken shenanigans. I didn't mean it either. Sure, I'm attracted to Daan, and I like everything about him. But 'love' is a bit of a stretch. It can't be. I've only known the man for a few weeks. My heart has not even healed yet from the love I've lost. I can't believe I said that to him. How embarrassing. How am I going to face him when he wakes up?

I look at Daan again, sleeping peacefully. It's hard to believe we've only met three weeks ago and started sleeping together just a week ago. It feels like a long time has passed since I embarrassed myself in front of him by falling off my bike, (me embarrassing myself in front of him has become a common theme at this point). It feels like we've known each other for a long time. Like we have so much history. How is it possible that we were complete strangers just a few weeks ago?

And this is gonna end in just a week. Next Monday, I'll go back to New York, and Daan and I will go back to being strangers. Maybe strangers who see each other once every few years because of Sophie. But strangers nonetheless. My life will not have Daan in it anymore. I don't know what that looks like. I don't know if I want that life.

Strangely, part of me believes that it would be harder to get used to a life without Daan than a life without Justin. A little part of me felt relieved when I walked away from Justin. Like a weight had been lifted off my shoulder and the nagging voice in my head had quietened. At the time, I thought it was because it was much better to find out about Justin being a cheater before we get married. But I'm not sure anymore. Maybe deep down, I've always known that Justin and I are not meant to be.

But with Daan, I have to walk away before even giving a chance to what we could be. It's like looking at the cover and synopsis of a book you really like and maybe even reading the preview and putting it down before reading it. Daan will remain my 'what if.' I have to walk away from all the joy he brought to my life. Daan might be the right guy for me. But he came into my life at the wrong time and wrong place.

Chapter Twenty-Four

"Oh my God, Bea. You're a lifesaver," I exclaim, holding the phone close to my ear. It's six in the morning. My friend, Beatriz, just called from New York to share the good news.

Beatriz is a grad student at New York University. We were introduced by a mutual friend a year ago, and we had coffee a few times. We're not the closest of friends, but we get along quite well.

When I heard last week that she was moving to Brazil for three months to complete her field research, I asked her if I could sublet her apartment. She said she would check with her landlord and get back to me. This phone call is her getting back to me with good news. The landlord confirmed that I can sublet her apartment. This will save me from staying on my mom's couch, at least for the time being. Bea's place is perfect for me. It's a small studio that I can afford without blowing through all my savings.

Daan looks at me, squinting his eyes while I talk to my friend. I feel bad that the phone call woke him up. I spent the night at his place, like I often do these days. Last night, we both passed out exhausted after making slow, passionate love. We savor every moment together these days, both of us realizing our time together is limited. We want to make the best of every last minute we have left.

"Sorry, I woke you up," I say, lying back down after I hang up the phone.

"No worries. What was that about?" he asks with a groggy voice.

"It's my friend Bea... the one I told you about. She said I can sublet her place."

"Great, I'm happy for you," he says, turning toward me to face me.

I smooth his eyebrow with my thumb, looking deeply into those blue eyes. "Thanks."

I smile widely, knowing that one of my worries has been resolved. But when I look into Daan's eyes, reality hits me, and my face dims. This is going to be over in just four days. After four days, I won't wake up next to Daan anymore. I won't be this close to him. I won't be able to touch him. The thought of that glooms my heart.

"What's wrong?" he asks, noticing the change on my face.

"The wedding is only three days away," I say quietly, my voice weak, barely above a whisper.

"Why does that make you sad?" he asks.

I know he understands why, and he doesn't need to hear the answer. I see the sadness on his face too. He just wants me to verbalize it for both of us.

"Because this is going to be over after that," I mumble, averting my gaze to escape his. Because if I keep looking at him, I don't think I can resist telling him that my heart doesn't want 'this' to be over.

It's painful to think about our impending deadline. Maybe not as painful as dealing with a long-distance relationship or risking heartbreak by choosing to be with a man who might still have feelings for his ex. Not as painful as allowing myself to trust another man after the man I trusted the most broke that trust. But still painful.

"This doesn't have to be over, you know," he says, looking down as if he needs to muster the courage to suggest it after I made it clear this wouldn't extend beyond two weeks.

"It has to, though," I say, my voice breaking a little. "Even if we decide to overlook the distance issue, I'm not ready to trust another man. Not yet."

"I know what Justin did was terrible. But you can't allow it to dictate the choices you make. You shouldn't give it that kind of power. You shouldn't make choices based on fear, Gem," he says, almost pleading.

"It's not just Justin, though," I retort, raising my voice a little higher.

"Other ex-boyfriends?" he asks calmly.

"Yes. But not just that. The first man to let me down was my dad. He left me and my mom when I was six. He just left like we meant nothing," I say, fighting back tears.

This is why I try to avoid talking about my dad. He was the first man to break my heart, and that heartbreak has never healed.

"I'm sorry, sweetheart," Daan says, running his hands through my hair.

"He's the one man who was supposed to love me unconditionally. But when things got hard, he left. I wasn't enough for him to fight through the difficult times. I wasn't enough to make him stay." Tears freely fall from my eyes now.

I don't share this with other people. I don't even think I shared this much with Justin. I just simply told him that my dad was not in the picture. But my dad is not just someone who is not in the picture. He's actually in the picture in all the horrible ways. He's there to remind me that men leave.

"What your dad did or what Justin did has nothing to do with you. It's on them. You could've done nothing differently to avoid that. You're more than enough," he says, looking deeply into my eyes as if he wants me to truly believe what he's saying. I know he means everything he says. But it's hard not to take things personally and truly believe that you're enough when the people who are supposed to love you treat you as less than.

Daan's words bring back what my mom always used to say whenever I insistently asked about my dad as a kid until I stopped. "Your dad loves you, honey. He just needs some things to work on, and it has nothing to do with you."

My mom never said anything bad about my dad. Now, looking back, I don't know how she did it. I don't know how she fought through the pain to share positive memories about my dad. She was left too. I'm sure she cried behind closed doors and cursed his name. But in front of me, my dad is a man who loves his daughter, not a man who left his family and never came back.

My mom's approach somehow backfired, though. As a child, I believed my dad loved me and would come back after he was done with the things he needed to work on. I waited for him to come back. But he never did. After years of waiting for him, one day, I woke up and accepted the reality that my dad was never coming back. That day, I stopped talking about him or asking about him. I compartmentalized his memory and the abandonment issues he left me with in the darkest corner of my brain.

"You know what the worst part is? I know he never tried to find me. Because if he did, he could've. We lived in the same apartment my whole life." I'm saying this out loud for the first time. I'm revisiting that dark corner of my brain and opening up.

Daan makes me feel safe and comfortable for some reason. I feel like I can talk to him about anything and share my fears and insecurities, and he listens with understanding on his face.

"Do you have any idea where he is?" he asks softly, his fingers drawing comforting circles on my arm.

"I heard he went back to his home country. My parents are both immigrants, and life hasn't been easy for them. But that's not enough reason to leave your family," I respond.

Daan remains quiet, giving me a space to process my feelings.

"So that coupled with what Justin did, who would blame me if I have major trust issues?" I add, forcing a laugh in an attempt to take away the heaviness and lighten the mood.

"No one can blame you. I wish I could take the pain away," he says, cradling my face and moving his thumb across my cheek.

I smile at him and give him a gentle kiss on the lips. "You've helped more than you know."

"Just so you know, this has never been just sex for me," he says, holding me close.

I've come to accept that we breached the 'just sex' rule as soon as we established it. What we've been doing in the past weeks is far from 'just sex.' I still plan to keep our arrangement temporary, but I know what we've become to each other is more than what we initially agreed upon.

I hide my face in the crook of his neck and say, "Neither for me."

We stay there for however long it is, just holding each other close. We both realize that even if this can't go on for long, the past few weeks have meant so much. Even if we can't

231

find a proper label for it, what we have is more than physical. It's 'more' in all possible ways.

"You said we have three more days?" he asks, holding my chin and lifting my face to look at me.

"Yeah."

He lifts me and puts me on top of him, allowing me to straddle him. "Let's make it count then."

"What do you have in mind?" I ask, grazing his lips with mine.

Daan has already taken this week off, and we've been inseparable for the last few days. I can't wait to spend the next three days with him.

"We'll date for three days. Not just sex. But real dating," he says, a smile flooding his face.

I beam at him. "I like that."

"Gemma, will you be my girlfriend for three days?"

"Yes, yes, a million times yes," I exclaim.

So, for the next three days, that's exactly what we do. We dress up and go out to dinners and movies. We have a romantic picnic at the park. We hit all the spots considered romantic in Amsterdam and beyond. We refer to each other as boyfriend and girlfriend when we meet new people. We slow dance in a piano bar. We link our hands over the table, dreamily gazing at each other. We talk about our childhood, our favorite everything, our hopes, and dreams. And we laugh, and laugh, and laugh until we get teary-eyed. We finish the night by making love. We make love like we're connected in all possible ways—mentally, emotionally, and physically. We make love in a way that says what we can't express with words.

In three days, we go on as many dates as most couples go on in three months and more. Those dates are the best dates I've ever been on. The amount of romance I feel in those three days surpasses the amount of romance I had in any of my previous relationships. By the end of the three days, I'm convinced more than ever that Daan is the right guy.

Chapter Twenty-Five

"Oh, you've already packed?" Daan says, looking at my slew of suitcases lined up in the living room.

I follow his gaze, placing a hand on my hips, admiring the result of my hard work. I managed to cram everything into the suitcases I came with, and I've bought a lot of new stuff here. I had to sit on them and grunt to zip them up, but I managed.

"Yeah, I won't have time to pack after the wedding," I say.

My flight is on Monday, the day after the wedding. I have to rush back to the apartment early Monday morning to grab my things, which doesn't give me enough time to pack or do anything else. Therefore, on Friday, I'm fully packed and ready before we leave for the wedding venue. Daan is here to pick me up for that. Close family members and everyone in the wedding party are staying at the venue for the whole weekend.

"Wow, it feels real now," he says without taking his eyes off my luggage.

I look at him. The sadness is palpable in his eyes and his whole demeanor. I'm sad too. I actually had to restrain myself from crying while I was packing earlier. It's bittersweet, but I don't know if it's more bitter than sweet.

On the one hand, I'm excited to get back to New York and get my business up and running. As much as I like my stay in Amsterdam, I miss New York. I miss the rush and bustle of the city. I miss my favorite bodega and the cat who open-ass sits on everything. (I have a conspiracy theory that she licks everything when no one is looking out of pure spite). Most of all, I miss my mom. I was used to seeing her at least once a week before I left New York. The only time I stayed this long without seeing my mom was when I lived in London for a year. So I'm excited to get back to my life.

On the other hand, I'm sad that I won't be with Daan anymore. I won't get to stare into those blue eyes until he averts his gaze. Getting back to my life means leaving behind the joy and love I found with Daan. I don't know if the feeling I have for Daan and what we shared over the past few weeks can be characterized as 'love,' but I don't have another word for it. What do you call it when you really like a person, are attracted to every part of their being, and admire everything they choose to be as a person? That's how I feel about Daan.

I can't keep pretending that there are no strings attached to this thing between Daan and me. There are strings that pull us toward each other. Strings that draw us together no matter how hard we try to stay apart—emotionally stay apart. I don't know if the strings are strong enough to keep us tied despite the distance and my inability to trust another guy. But they're there.

Now, as I see him standing here in front of me, his face burdened by the weight of our circumstances, I feel an overwhelming need to tell him how much I value our time together, how much I value him. I wrap my arms around his waist, pressing my chin to his chest as I look up at him, but he's still not meeting my gaze.

"Daan," I call his name softly to get his attention.

"Yeah," he says with a hoarse voice, finally looking at me. He cradles my face with his hands.

"My leaving is real. But what we've been to each other is also real, no matter how brief it might have been. At least, it's all real for me," I say, fighting back the tears prickling my eyes.

"It's all real for me too," he replies, leaning in to gently take my lips with his.

He kisses me slowly and intentionally, as if he's conveying something profound. This kiss speaks volumes. It says everything we might not have the courage to verbalize to each other. It communicates our love and fear—fear of losing each other, fear of not being together anymore, fear that this genuine connection might not endure beyond two days.

***

As we arrive at the venue, I fully embrace my wedding planner persona. I'm darting around with a clipboard in hand, ticking off tasks and issuing instructions to the decorators and vendors. I make calls until my ears ring to make sure that everything is in order for Sunday. I have convinced Sophie to hire a wedding day coordinator since I'm part of the wedding party and won't be able to keep an eye on everything.

Sophie couldn't care less about the details. I'm practically in charge of everything at this point. When I try to brief her about the specific details, she waves me off, saying, "I don't really care about having the perfect wedding. I just want to have a big party where everyone can have fun and get loose." And she shimmies her shoulders to demonstrate what getting loose looks like. So I'm on my own. Unlike her, I deeply care about her having the perfect wedding. I don't want anything major to go wrong.

My control freak and planner self can't fathom how she's not obsessing about every little detail. I'm obsessing over every little detail, and it's not even my wedding. Case in point: I just spent thirty minutes trying to correct a crooked flower arrangement at some random corner of the venue probably no one would even notice.

I also boss around poor Daan to help me with some things. And he does it with a smile on his face. I don't know how he's not already tired of me or doesn't think I'm a freak. I'd think I'm a freak if I looked at myself from the outside.

On Saturday, the wedding planning reaches its heights, and I've been at it since dawn. I even forget to eat even if there is catering for breakfast, lunch, and dinner for those staying at the venue. I spend most part of the day helping the venue decorator—by helping, I mean bossing her around and telling her what to do. I feel like it will all crumble down if I take my eyes off it for a second.

I know deep down that this is not just about Sophie's wedding at this point. I'm also trying to prove to myself, more than anyone else, that I can do this event planning thing and make a career out of it. I'm taking this as a test or even a sign. As if the success of this wedding could determine the success of the business I haven't even started yet. So, for me, the stakes of this wedding are way high.

Around four in the afternoon, I see Daan walking toward me with a purpose while I'm nagging one of the workers for the hundredth time.

"Come with me," he instructs, holding my hand and tugging me without even giving me a chance to respond.

I see the worker I'm talking to take advantage of the interruption and scurry away. He must be praying for someone to take me away. Little did he know that I won't be leaving this site for even a minute today.

"Where?...no...I have to stay here and help," I protest.

But Daan doesn't stop. "No, you don't. You have to come with me. It's not a request," he says firmly, still holding my hand and tugging me.

"You can't force me to do anything." I stop before we take the stairs that lead to the rooms.

I see a mischievous grin build up at the corner of his mouth. "Watch me."

Before I can register what is happening, he scoops me up the ground and carries me up the stairs. I'm angry and a little turned on at the same time. What is he gonna do to me? The part of my brain that stays in the gutter tries to play out possible fantasies. *Stop you weak-link, this is not acceptable. No one should carry me without my consent*, I yell at myself internally.

Daan takes me to his room. And when he puts me down, I glare at him with absolute fury. If he thinks he can charm his way out of this after pulling this alpha male crap, he's got another thing coming. Hell no! I don't let anyone get away with that, not even Daan.

"How dare…" I start, looking up at him and wagging my finger furiously.

"Eat," he interrupts me calmly, pointing at the table behind me.

That's when I turn around and see the table full of delicious-looking food, which makes me realize how hungry I am. I haven't eaten anything the whole day and my stomach grumbles just at the sight of food.

My energy immediately changes. My rage is replaced by a weak smile. This is very thoughtful. I'm touched.

"Oh…Daan…this is so nice," I say. I feel like crying. God, my emotions are all over the place these days.

"I know you'd forgive me for forcing you here if I feed you," he grins.

"You know me too well," I say, sitting down to dig into the feast spread in front of me. Once again, I'm fully enamored by Daan's thoughtfulness.

Chapter Twenty-Six

By the end of the day, everything seems in order and ready for tomorrow. And I'm finally able to breathe. After dinner, all the bridesmaids gather in Sophie's room to toast to the final night of her singledom. Sophie is wearing a white silk robe, which she jokingly says represents her final night of innocence. The rest of us are wearing light blue robes gifted to us by the bride. It's not lost on me that we look like we're in a cult, with Sophie being the cult leader. Then again, if anyone has the charismatic and convincing personality of a cult leader, it would be Sophie. But only in a good way.

We sit around the bride, practically reciting our unwavering devotion to her and her wedding day. The expensive champagne is flowing, and everyone is having a good time. Sima is making us laugh, telling one of her crazy stories. This time, she was talking about the time she found out that her ex-boyfriend was cheating on her. So, in a typical Sima fashion, she decided to take matters into her own hands. She changed his password on some of his accounts, practically locking him out for weeks. She also shared his streaming service logins with random people. It took him a while to realize why the streaming platforms were telling him to continue watching random shows he hadn't even started. Also, that messed up his algorithm for quite some time.

We crack up at Sima's absolute pettiness. The guy deserved it, but it takes a certain level of commitment to mess with someone for an extended period. Sima is that committed.

"Oh, this is fun. Does anyone else have other petty revenge stories?" Sophie asks, looking around the room.

"I'm not proud of it, but I have one," Paige responds sheepishly.

We all look at her in surprise. Paige is always the 'take the high road' type of person. She even often scolds Sima for being petty and choosing to fight. So, no one expected petty stories from her.

"Oh, do tell, you sneaky little Petty Crocker," Sophie says, tilting her head and raising one of her eyebrows.

"Okay, it was when I was in uni. I had this roommate who was really difficult to live with. She stole my food, didn't clean up after herself, and always talked loudly in the middle of the night. So, I started to mess with her...mess with her reality, to be precise," Paige says villainously.

"Mess with her reality how?" I ask, not sure if I want to know the answer.

"Like moving things around the apartment and acting surprised when she asked me if I moved them, turning the lights on and off when she thought I was not home, making weird sounds...things like that. And I looked at her like she was crazy when she brought it up. After a couple of months, she was convinced that the apartment was haunted. So, she moved out, and I lived happily ever after," she explains, laughing.

We all look at her with wide eyes and gaping mouths. Who would've thought Paige had this in her? Messing with someone for months.

"Wow, that's harsh, Paige," Sima says. If Sima thinks it's harsh, it's really harsh.

"I said I'm not proud of it. Plus, she really was a horrible roommate, and I had to be creative," Paige retorts.

Just then, Julia leans in close to my ear and whispers, "Can I talk to you outside for a minute?"

What now? I honestly don't know what she wants at this point. All our interactions so far have been unpleasant. I was actually hoping to stay the heck away from her until this wedding was over. I mentally prepare myself for another unpleasant conversation and follow her to the balcony, leaving the bridal suite.

I stand against the parapet facing her and wait for her to speak. Her expression is unreadable, but she doesn't look angry or bitter like the last couple of times we spoke.

"I just wanted to say sorry," she says sheepishly.

This is different. Am I hearing this right? I let her continue without responding.

"I've been kind of a bitch to you since the first day we met. I didn't even admit it to myself at the beginning. I told

242

myself we're just different people and we don't get along. I think I haven't been honest with myself."

"About what?" I ask.

"To be completely honest, I saw how Daan looks at you and how he's around you...and I felt threatened," she says, sounding as though this is the most difficult thing she has to admit out loud.

I want to stay mad at her, but I know that she's being sincere. Her attitude toward me hasn't been great, to put it mildly. She acted from a place of insecurity, which I understand. What I don't understand is why she even cares so much about a guy she fell out of love with. I know it's not ideal to see her ex getting closer to another person, but it wouldn't be hard to ignore if she didn't care about him.

"Thank you for the apology; I appreciate it. But what I don't understand is why you felt threatened. You're not still in love with him, right?" I ask.

She remains silent for a moment, as if she's contemplating what she wants to share. "I don't know. I mean...I don't think I've ever stopped loving him. And lately, I feel like I made a mistake by breaking up with him."

My heart sinks a little. If she decides to go back to him, would he take her back? I know it's not reasonable to expect Daan not to be with her or anyone else when I can't be with him. And I won't even be around to see any of it. But the thought of him with her or someone else still stings a little.

"I thought you broke up with him because you fell out of love," I say more like a statement than a question.

"That's what I told him, but not really. It's more like I felt like we got too complacent, and the relationship was not exciting anymore," she says with a clear sadness in her voice. "But I now realize that we got comfortable with each other like we didn't have to try to impress each other anymore. That's different from being complacent, and being comfortable in a long-term relationship is not really a bad thing."

I'm not sure if I should tell her about the arrangement between Daan and me. I don't think it's my place to tell her. Daan should be the one to tell her. But I also don't want to be the reason for them to be apart if they both want to get back together.

"But it doesn't matter. I have no intention of getting between you two. He actually looks happier, and I want him to be happy no matter what," she adds, interrupting my train of thought.

The last part resonates with me the most. I want Daan to be happy too. If getting back with Julia makes him happy, which I believe it would, I'm not going to stand in the way of that.

"Actually...what's going on between Daan and me is not what you think. We're not really together-together," I say, hesitating to say this out loud.

She looks at me, confused. So I explain. "You were not far off when you said I'm using him as a holiday pastime. I'm not using him per se. But we have an arrangement."

Then I tell her about Daan and my 'relationship' and what it entails. I don't tell her every single detail, but I tell her the parts she needs to know. I see a smile spread across her face, a realization dawning on her that she's not too late to get Daan back, while I feel my heart sink to the bottom.

Chapter Twenty-Seven

I look at my reflection in the mirror. I'm wearing a sleeveless green bridesmaid's dress. The scoop neckline and side slit flatter my figure, if I may say so myself. My curls are freshly styled and pinned to the side. I smile at my reflection, parting my lips painted with brown lipstick.

Sophie appears behind me. She looks breathtaking in her custom-made sweetheart neckline wedding dress. With her tall and slender frame, she looks like she's modeling the dress. The minimal makeup and hairstyle she's chosen accentuate all her attractive features.

I turn around to gush over the beautiful bride. "Oh, Soph, you look beautiful."

"I know," she says honestly, a smile taking over her face.

When it's time for the wedding ceremony, we leave the bridal suite crowding the bride. The groomsmen are waiting for us by the gate. My heart jumps when I see Daan. He looks extra handsome in his navy blue tux. As our eyes meet, I see a smile spreading across his face and his mouth gaping slightly. It's like the world around us has stopped, and we can only see each other.

"You look beautiful," he whispers in my ear when I go to stand next to him.

He looks like he wants to kiss me. He leans in, but he hesitates mid-way, I assume, when he realizes that we're not alone. We're surrounded by the whole wedding party. Instead, he lightly winks at me.

"You look great too," I whisper back, linking my arm in his. We're walking down the aisle together.

Daan and I are the first to walk down the aisle, followed by the other pairs of bridesmaids and groomsmen. After we take our assigned spots, I subtly signal to the wedding coordinator to cue the band to play the song Sophie and Lucas have chosen. Then, Sophie walks down the aisle gracefully with a big smile on her face, accompanied by both of her parents.

The wedding ceremony passes like a whirlwind. I meet Daan's eyes when Sophie and Lucas recite their vows. We lock eyes for a while and share weak smiles in some form of non-verbal communication. I don't really hear the vows, not only because they're in Dutch, but also because my attention is fixed on Daan. On what he means to me and what our lives and future would look like if there weren't so many reasons why we can't be together. Would we be standing in Sophie and Lucas's place? Would we find our happily ever after in each other?

Standing here, I'm overwhelmed by a bittersweet feeling. I'm extremely happy for Sophie. Seeing her stepping into the next stage of her life with so much excitement brings me immense joy. On the other hand, this is my last day with Daan. I'm flying back to New York tomorrow. I know this is what I signed up for, but I have this sinking feeling in the pit of my stomach. I feel a mix of sadness, uncertainty, and impending regret.

***

Sophie gets the wedding she wanted: everyone having fun, eating, drinking, and dancing with no limits. The food is delicious, and the open bar keeps everyone happy. My first attempt at wedding planning is proving to be a success. I know I didn't plan this wedding from the beginning, but the tasks I've worked on have been successful. It's giving me the boost I need going into my event planning business.

At some point, Sophie waves me over to one of the family tables. She's talking to an older woman dressed head-to-toe in Chanel. The woman looks like she's in her mid-fifties. She's sitting all prim and proper, sipping out of her tall champagne glass.

"This is my aunt Linda. She was raving about the wedding, so I thought I should introduce her to my bridesmaid-slash-visionary wedding planner," Sophie says, giving me a knowing smile.

The woman flashes me her expensive-looking veneers. Her smile is restrained and measured, but still polite.

Honestly, I don't know if I can take all the credit for the wedding planning. A significant portion of it had been taken care of by the previous wedding planner before I took over. Even then, I believe my role has been helping Sophie with the wedding planning rather than being the actual wedding planner. Then again, Sophie believed in my judgment and gave me the liberty to make a lot of crucial decisions.

In any case, I don't know where Sophie is going with this introduction, so I don't say anything. I just smile back at the fancy woman.

"Linda lives in New York, and she's looking for an event planner to plan her daughter's sixteenth birthday party, which will take place in the Hamptons. I thought you would be perfect for the job," Sophie says, shifting her gaze between the woman and me.

"Sophie tells me you also live in New York, Gemma. Do you have a minute to chat, and we can take it from there?" Linda asks.

She has this posh way of speaking that immediately intimidates me, but I'm excited at the same time. She could be my first client for my business that hasn't even been registered yet. I need to play my cards right to convince this woman that I'm the perfect event planner for her daughter's sweet sixteen party, despite not having planned a similar event before.

"Of course, I'd be happy to chat," I say with my utmost professional tone.

"I'll leave you two to it," Sophie says, kissing Aunt Linda on the cheek. She then gives me a hug and whispers in my ear, "She's loaded; don't understate your fee."

Based on our short chat, Linda seems like a woman who knows exactly what she wants and has very high standards for any service she requests. She also seems like someone who likes to be in control and wants to be involved in every part of the process, unlike Sophie. It's a bit intimidating, but I can work with that. And there's no doubt that she's loaded. The birthday celebration she has in mind is so big that it puts many weddings to shame. It seems like she doesn't care about the budget; she just wants to give her daughter and her friends the biggest celebration ever.

She asks me to prepare a pitch with ideas for the party and meet with her in New York as soon as possible. Of course, I agree with the greatest enthusiasm. We decide to meet next Friday for a pitch meeting, and if I nail the pitch, I'll get the job. I have to nail the pitch, no question about it.

With the excitement of the wedding and potentially scoring my first client, I can't wipe the smile off my face. I just stand in the corner, taking it all in and grinning like a total weirdo. I probably need some time to completely reflect on my experience in the past month, but I can't help getting choked up thinking about how far I've come. The universe really has its own way of teaching you. The lesson might be delivered in a harsh way, but the reward is priceless.

"Can I have this dance?" I hear the deep voice I'm too familiar with ask.

'Thinking Out Loud' by Ed Sheeran is playing, and Daan is standing in front of me, holding out his hand to me. I take it, and we head to the middle of the dance floor.

As the heartwarming music fills the air, we link hip to hip, chest to chest, and slowly sway following the rhythm. I feel Daan's hand on the small of my back, his warmth protruding through the thin silk material of my dress. I grip his neck with both arms, drawing him close. Our touch is gentle, our gaze meaningful.

The lyrics of the song draw so much emotion out of me. Daan and I might not have the opportunity to love each other until we're seventy. But the time we spent together is meaningful. What we feel for each other means something, even if I don't have the word for it. Daan means so much to me.

My eyes prick with tears, but I don't avert my gaze. He doesn't break eye contact either.

"What's wrong?" he asks with a weak voice. But I'm pretty sure he knows what's wrong. I don't have to tell him. I just shrug, my eyes filling with tears even more.

I see the same emotion go through his eyes. "I know," he says, as if he knows what I'm thinking and what's making me emotional. "This sucks," his voice breaks a little. We both realize that this is going to be our last dance.

Chapter Twenty-Eight

"We're sneaking out," Sophie whispers in my ear with childlike enthusiasm.

It's way into the night, but it seems like the party is just getting started. Everyone is mingling, drinking, and dancing with full energy. So, imagine my surprise when the 'I-want-everyone-to-get-loose-and-have-fun' herself wants to sneak out of her own wedding party. I mean, who sneaks out of their own wedding?

"Why?" I exclaim, my surprise palpable in my tone.

"We're exhausted, and we want to have some time alone together just to take everything in," she responds, looking adoringly at Lucas. He winks at her in what looks like a private conversation between the two.

"You don't have to sneak out though. You can just say your goodbyes and give everyone an opportunity to officially send you off," I retort, my wedding planner side taking over.

Sophie squeezes my hand conspiratorially. "We want everyone to stay as long as they want and party. We don't want them to take our departure as a sign of the end of the party."

I smile at her. I'm back to being a bridesmaid and a friend again. Whatever Sophie wants, she gets. So, I sneak them out through the back door that the vendors have been using without anyone noticing. Everyone is too drunk to notice anyway.

"Walk with me to my room; I have something to give you," Sophie tells me as soon as we get to the hallway.

I shoot her a puzzled look. "What is it?"

"You'll see," she says, walking to the honeymoon suite with her arm linked to Lucas's.

"You did an amazing job with the wedding, Gemma. It's everything we wanted and more," Lucas tells me with absolute sincerity.

I'm overjoyed to hear this from him. Being not an expressive person like Sophie is, I know he doesn't give compliments easily. So when he says, 'I did an amazing job with the wedding,' I know he means it. I pocket this validation with the others I've received throughout the day. I'll open the pocket and revisit them when I have bad days with my business; when I feel like an imposter; when I have doubts about what I can do.

"Thank you," I say. I'm overwhelmed by all the positive responses I've received about the wedding. It's giving me the confidence I need going into my event planning business.

When we get to the suite, Lucas goes directly to the bedroom, giving us some privacy. I stand in the living area with a mix of confusion and curiosity while Sophie fishes some kind of paper from her bag. She hands me the paper, smiling widely.

When I glance at it, I notice it's a bank statement. I look up at her, still confused. She gestures for me to read it, pointing her chin to the statement I'm holding. So I do. It's a fifty-grand deposit to my bank account.

"What's this, Soph?" I ask, still not understanding why Sophie deposited all this money in my bank account.

"It's a little something to help you start your business," she says, still smiling widely.

"I can't accept this. This is too much," I say, emotions swirling within me.

She holds my hands. "I know you want to do this by yourself, and I respect that. So it's an interest-free loan that you can pay me back at any time."

My eyes cloud with tears. This is one of the most thoughtful things anyone has ever done for me. It's not just about the money. Sophie knows my needs without me telling her, and she extends her helping hand graciously without me even asking. She did that when she invited me to come to Amsterdam, let me live in her apartment rent-free, and gave me the opportunity to plan her wedding, reigniting my passion to start my own event planning business.

"I don't know what to say. Thank you," I mutter, letting my tears fall.

As much as I pride myself on my independence and my ability to pull myself up by my bootstraps when life knocks me down, I also recognize that sometimes we all need someone to pick us up when we're too tired to get up. Too fed up to fight. Too down to see the light at the end of the tunnel. Sophie has been that person for me.

She gives me a tight hug. "You deserve it. You actually should've sent me a bill for your wedding planning fee." She laughs, breaking the emotional heaviness.

I laugh too, my eyes still misty. "Not when I'm living in your apartment for free and being chauffeured around by your brother."

"Your business is gonna grow so much before you know it, Gem. I can almost see you being the biggest event planner in New York," she says, gesturing to an imaginary title written in the sky.

"I want to believe you. But the statistics show that a large portion of new businesses struggle to survive in the first few years," I respond.

I want to be realistic and set the right expectations. I'm committed more than ever to starting my business and working as hard as I can. But I'm in no way delusional enough to think that failure is not a possibility. There is so much risk and uncertainty when it comes to starting a new business. But this time around, I'm ready to embrace the risk and uncertainty.

"Fuck the statistics. I know you. I know how hard you work and how obsessive you get. Look at what you did with my wedding in such a limited time. I'm sure you're not gonna be part of the depressing statistics," she says with her usual sunny attitude.

I give her another hug, both to show my gratitude and as a goodbye. I won't have a chance to see her again before I leave tomorrow. I'm going to miss her more than ever. Sophie and I have always been close since we met on that wet autumn day in London, but the last month has brought us even closer.

This trip has really turned out to be a journey of self-discovery and healing in the best way possible. I've healed—or at least started the process of healing—and (re)discovered myself and my passion. I can finally fully see the silver lining in the events that turned my life upside down and pushed me out of New York. Ironically, I reached my destination by running away from my problems. There really is a light at the end of the tunnel. I owe it to Sophie for suggesting that I come to Amsterdam and for pushing me to practically plan her wedding.

Just as I start walking out of the door, Sophie calls out after me, "And Gem…"

I turn around.

"Maybe take a leap of faith with Daan as well," she says, flashing me a knowing smile.

"You knew?" I ask hesitantly, walking back toward her. I didn't tell her about Daan and me. I don't think he has told her, either. He would have told me if he did.

"From the way you guys ogle each other, anyone can see it… let alone me, who knows both of you closely."

I cover my face, feeling half embarrassed and half relieved that she knows. I've been feeling bad for hiding this from her. There's not much she doesn't know about my life, and it has been tough not telling her everything about Daan— how I feel about him, how he makes me feel.

"You thought you were being slick, huh?" she adds, laughing.

"I'm sorry, Soph. I didn't mean to keep things from you. It's just weird to talk to you about sleeping with your brother," I blush uncontrollably.

"I get it. My brother's sex life is the last thing I want to hear about. But I have a feeling that this thing between you is more than that, even if you don't see it now."

I don't say anything. I don't think I disagree with her. These past few days, I've been feeling that this thing between Daan and me is far from 'just sex.' I don't know who and what we can be to each other, but he means a lot to me. He came to me at one of the darkest times of my life, and he put a smile back on my face. Being with Daan has been healing more than anyone could imagine. I don't believe in a rebound, and I never considered Daan as my rebound. But if a rebound means someone who helps one through heartbreak and healing, he has been that for me.

Maybe Sophie is right. Maybe I should take a leap of faith with Daan.

I give my friend another tight hug and rush out to the reception hall. I need to see Daan. I don't know what I want to say to him, but I need to see him.

I stand by the door of the reception hall and look around, trying to locate Daan. Then, I see him on the dance floor. He's dancing with Julia. They're very close to each other. He has his hand on her lower back, like he did with me just less than an hour ago. She has her hand on his shoulder. They are gazing at each other, smiling. She's closer in height to him that she doesn't even have to crane her neck to look at him like I do.

I freeze in place and stare at them. They are lost in each other's eyes that they don't see me. I don't think they see anyone around them. Like the way I felt when I danced with him earlier; I felt like we were the only ones in the room. They must be feeling the same thing. And they have so much history that their eye contact carries a lot of weight. I wonder if they can read what they had been and what they could be together in each other's eyes. I wonder if they are being reminded of the love they had for each other. The love they never really got over. I wonder if they communicate more than they could in words when they stare at each other like that.

I know I shouldn't be jealous, but seeing them like this sinks my heart. Maybe they are meant to be together. Maybe my role here is to remind Julia what Daan means to her. To remind her of the love she still has for him. Maybe my place in Daan's life is to bring the love of his life back to him. Julia's words echo in my head, "I want Daan to be happy." I also want Daan to be happy. Maybe my way of making Daan happy is to let him reexplore things with Julia.

Having that talk with him right now, when I don't know if I can fully let him into my life, might not be a good idea. I'll only mess with his head. How can I do that to him when I don't even know what I want? When I don't know if I can make space for him in my life right now? That's not what a person who wants happiness for another person would do. Daan doesn't deserve someone who is not ready to fully trust him and wholeheartedly try. He deserves someone who is ready to love him. Maybe Julia is that person. She has already learned how horrible losing Daan is. I'm pretty sure she would do anything not to lose him again.

I see Julia whisper something in his ear and head to the balcony. He follows her. Maybe this doesn't even mean anything, but it reminds me of all the reasons why I shouldn't try with Daan. It brings back all the reasons why we can't be together. And nothing has changed. Those reasons still stand. I turn around and walk away.

Chapter Twenty-Nine

I sit at the airport, grappling with a mix of emotions running through my head. I'm excited to return to New York and get my business up and running. When it comes to my new career move, things have been working out better than I expected. My business proposal and strategy are fully written and ready. I've even designed my own business logo based on my limited graphic design knowledge. I also have the initial capital to start the business and my first potential client. Looking back, my time in Amsterdam has been life-changing.

But I feel deeply sad as I sit here waiting for my flight. Sad that I don't have the courage to pursue things with Daan. That I'm afraid to risk another heartbreak by trusting another person. That I'm not ready to let another man into my life, no matter how great he is. I'm sad that the people who hurt me in the past have left me guarded and cagey and that they have a lasting effect on me. I know healing from these scars takes time. It's not something that can happen in just a month.

When I left yesterday, I didn't look back. I didn't even allow myself to question my decision. As soon as I left the reception hall, I went back to my room, quickly grabbed my things, and just left. Fortunately, I found some wedding guests who had a car service to Amsterdam, and they gave me a ride.

I feel like a coward for leaving without saying goodbye to Daan. But I didn't have the courage to face him. I was afraid that I'd break down. If I'm fully honest with myself, I was afraid that if I saw his face one more time, I'd change my mind and decide to stay or do something equally unreasonable.

I hope the little note I quickly scribbled and left in his room could tell him what I couldn't tell him in person. I hope he knows how much I appreciate him. How much he means to me.

Daan,

I'm sorry I left without saying goodbye. I'm just not good at goodbyes. Plus, I thought the last dance we shared was the perfect ending to the perfect time we had together.

You brought so much joy and peace to one of the darkest times of my life. You mean so much to me. What we had has been 'more' to me.

I wish you all the happiness in life.

Till next time,

G.

It's been six hours since I left the note. I wonder if he's gotten it by now. If he returned to his room after the party ended, he probably has. I hope he doesn't feel betrayed or disregarded, as if someone broke up with him via text. I know this isn't a breakup. But I also understand that the least I could've done for Daan is look him in the eyes, thank him for the wonderful time we had together, and bid a proper farewell. I just didn't have the courage.

I don't know if he tried to find me or contact me after discovering the note. I left the venue immediately after and discarded my Dutch phone number. I'm currently using my American number, which he doesn't know, or at least as far as I know. So even if he tries, he has no means to reach me.

I'm aware that running away like this seems to be becoming a pattern for me. But I believe this is the right decision. I'm following through with my well-thought-out plan. This is the arrangement Daan and I agreed upon. Yet, I feel something tugging at my heart, as if I'm making the biggest mistake of my life. I'm going home, but it feels like I'm running away from one.

I need to talk to someone and unload whatever I'm feeling. I can't bother Sophie now. So, I call Sima.

"Hey, Gem," Sima says, her voice groggy like she just woke up. I feel bad for waking her. She's probably hungover too.

"Sorry, Sim. Can you talk?" I ask hesitantly.

"Yeah, I can summon my two brain cells to talk. What's up?"

"I left Daan. I didn't even say goodbye," I blurt out, my voice cracking a little.

Sima stays silent, giving me a space to gather my thoughts and continue.

"I'm so conflicted and overwhelmed by all these crazy emotions. I don't even know why. I'm going back home without trying with Daan. You know…actually trying," I attempt to articulate my jumbled-up thoughts.

"That's what you wanted, right?" Sima says softly.

"Yeah. But why does it feel like I left a part of me behind?" I feel frustrated with myself. This is supposed to be the right thing to do. This is what I signed up for. It's been the plan all along. So why the hell do I feel like I'm making one of the biggest mistakes of my life?

"Maybe because you love him?" she says; her tone holds a mix of statement and a question.

"How?" I ask. "I was in love and engaged to be married to another man just a month ago. Is it even possible to fall in love when I haven't fully recovered from the love I've lost? How is this love?"

"You can't plan when love comes into your life, Gem. Maybe falling in love is part of your healing," Sima responds empathetically.

I'm surprised to hear this from her. She's not often the soppy romantic type. She's pragmatic, through and through. It's unlike her to believe that people can fall in love after only knowing each other for a few weeks. It's unlike her to suggest that people should overlook all the realistic reasons why they shouldn't be together for the sake of love. She doesn't usually think love can overcome everything. I called her, hoping she'd talk me off the ledge and tell me to stop crying and get my ass on the plane.

"What am I going to do now? Even if I decide to overlook the distance, how do I know he wouldn't break my heart like Justin?" I say quietly.

I don't want to go through a horrible breakup again. I don't want to feel like I'm not enough. Not having love is much better than losing it in a way that shatters your sense of self.

"You don't know. You just have to decide whether you want to embrace the uncertainty and take a chance on love."

I know she's not wrong. There is no certainty about what the future holds, especially when it comes to love. We don't know if people are who we think they are. We don't know if people would change. We don't know if the people who love us dearly today hate our guts tomorrow. We just have to take a leap and hope for the best. But I don't know if I'm ready for that. I'm scared to embrace the unknown when it comes to my heart.

Chapter Thirty

"There are plenty of workspaces here and upstairs," the leasing agent, giving me a tour of the coworking space, Tony, says. It's Friday at noon, and this is the second coworking space I've viewed today.

I scan the room, looking at the different working desks and chairs scattered around the room, and the coffee machine and the water cooler in the corner. It's decorated with modern furniture with inviting bright colors. The room has floor-to-ceiling windows that brighten the place and offer a nice view of the New York City skyline.

Renting an independent office space in New York City is way over my budget. Plus, I don't necessarily need that at this stage. I just need a place to work in peace and hold meetings with my clients. So, I decided to go for one of those coworking spaces. I'm already inspired when I see many entrepreneurs utilizing the space and working on their craft.

Tony leads me to the next room. "This is the breakroom; we normally call it 'the zen room'," he says, keeping his voice down.

When I see the woman with a bright red hair sitting on a bean bag in the corner of the room and meditating, I understand why the volume of his voice changed. Bright-colored bean bags are placed all over the room. There are also comfortable-looking couches and armchairs around the room. I see a chessboard on one of the coffee tables.

I already like this place. I like it better than the place I viewed earlier, which felt cramped and stuffy. I can see myself working and socializing here. As luck would have it, this working space has a couple of openings, and I'm hoping my application will be accepted. Tony has already assured me that, most likely, it will.

"Let me show you the conference rooms," he says, walking ahead of me.

I follow him to the corridor. He opens one of the doors lining up on the different sides of the corridor and gestures for me to get inside. It's a small conference room that can accommodate a maximum of eight people.

"We have different conference and meeting rooms of different sizes. The biggest one can host around twenty people," he says. "You can use these rooms whenever you have a meeting. Just make sure to book in advance using the online form."

I nod, looking around the room. This is perfect for me. I only need a meeting room to meet with clients and vendors. Since I don't have staff, I don't need a big conference room.

"This place is amazing. I really like it. It's certainly what I'm looking for," I tell him.

It has been five days since I returned to New York. I was welcomed by the city, fully blooming with mid-spring weather. The energy engulfed me as soon as I stepped into the busy JFK airport. I breathed in the chaotic scene taking place around me and the rush of the city that never sleeps. I didn't realize how much I missed this city until I was reminded why I love it so much. At the risk of falling into a cliché, it's the energy. There is no other way to explain it. It's the best place for me, and I plan to live here until my end days. New York is home. It has always been.

Getting on that plane, however, was one of the hardest things I've ever done. I practically had to force myself to board the plane after they announced the final boarding call. I had to fight my urge to run across the airport like a rom-com star and go to wherever Daan was.

In the last four days, I've been running around to get the groundwork for my new business. I started the business registration process, viewed some office spaces, and printed out some business cards. Holding my business card in my hand made it feel like it's all real. I have a business now.

In the evening, I head to my meeting with Linda, Sophie's aunt and my first potential client. I feel a mix of excitement and nervousness as I walk from the subway station to her house. I need to get this job. She's my only client, and I plan to use this event as an opportunity to connect with other potential clients. So, a lot is riding on this meeting.

Linda emailed me information about her daughter, Grace, a couple of days ago—what she likes, what she doesn't like, and all that. Grace is very much into space, and her dream is to be an astronaut. So I prepared a pitch for a galaxy-themed party, but very high-end. My PowerPoint presentation is filled with 3D mockups, pictures, and all the selling points of my services. If this doesn't impress her, I don't know what would.

Linda lives in a fancy apartment building on Fifth Avenue on the Upper East Side. I don't have to say much else to express how wealthy she is. Her gigantic penthouse overlooks Central Park and the New York skyline. She's a single mother and lives with only her daughter in this apartment that can house all the Brady Bunch and their descendants.

To my surprise, Linda is such a pleasant and welcoming person. I thought she was uptight and snobby when I first met her at Sophie's wedding. She didn't talk much at the wedding, and she had this air of superiority to her, at least that was what I thought. I was fearing that she might not be the most pleasant person to work with. But it turns out she's down-to-earth and lovely.

She tells me that Grace's dad passed away a couple of years ago, and it's been very hard on Grace. This is the first birthday she's agreed to celebrate after her dad passed, she tells me. Linda really wants to give her a one-of-a-kind experience, an extravagant party where she can have fun with her friends.

"She's such a good kid," Linda says, her face beaming with pride. She tells me that Grace is a straight-A student who spends most of her time with her head in her books than partying. This gives me more ideas for the party; I'll embrace Grace's nerdy side.

Linda doesn't put as much weight into the pitch as I expected. It appears that she has already decided to hire me after Sophie vouched for me, and she just wanted to see what ideas I could come up with. Her face lights up when I explain my galaxy-themed party.

"Grace would love this," she says, her wide smile coating her face. This is the first time I've seen her smiling from ear to ear like this, and I internally pat myself on the back for the job well done.

So I get the job. I feel like jumping around when I leave the apartment. Things are working better than I expected, and I'm beyond grateful. I even smile and say "hi" to strangers on the street who are minding their own business. Some say "hi" back with a confused look on their faces, and others give me a side-eye. But I don't care. I'm having a great day. I still don't know much about where to start with actually planning the event and hiring different vendors for a birthday party. But I'll figure it out. That's one thing I know I'm good at. Figuring it out.

***

When I get home—by home, I mean Bea's apartment that I'm subletting—I receive a strange text from Sophie. *Please don't be mad at me. I had to do it.*

Do what? I text back.

My phone dings again. *You'll see.*

I can't think of anything she could've done that would make me mad, especially when we are thousands of miles apart.

But the text immediately transports me right back to Daan. I've been trying not to think about him since I left Amsterdam and failing miserably. I can't help thinking about what he's doing, what he's feeling. I think about him doing his day-to-day mundane activities. I think about him being here with me and watching me when I do my mundane day-to-day activities. I wonder if he thinks of me. Does he think of me first thing in the morning like I do every morning? Does he fall asleep replaying the wonderful time we had together like I do every night?

While I'm daydreaming about all things Daan, I hear my doorbell ring. Who could it be? Not many people know my current address, and I like to keep it that way.

I open the door absentmindedly, not expecting much. Nothing could've prepared me for what—or rather, who—I see standing in front of me. It's Daan. Daan is standing right at my door. I blink, close and open my eyes again to ensure he's not just a figment of my imagination. He's really here, flesh and blood.

I freeze where I stand. I'm stunned. I just stare into his eyes—his gorgeous blue eyes. I look at his hesitant smile. He's smiling like he's not sure about how I feel about him showing up at my place across the Atlantic unannounced. I know I should speak to ease his worry, but I'm left speechless.

"Daan," is all I can manage to say before I throw myself on him.

He holds me against his chest, close to his fast-beating heart, matching my own heart racing uncontrollably. I hold onto him tightly as if trying to make up for all the times I've missed him, for all the times I've thought about him, for all the times I've wished he was here.

We stand there, wrapped in each other's embrace, for what feels like an eternity. Neither of us speaks. But his hug says everything. It tells me that he's missed me too; that he's thought about me too; that he's wished he was with me too.

We step inside, closing the door behind us. That's when we break away just enough to gaze into each other's eyes.

"What are you doing here?" I ask softly, attempting to hold back my emotions.

"I came to see you. I needed to see you," he responds, his voice breaking a little, in a way that tells me that he's also feeling the overwhelming longing and adoration I'm feeling.

He gently tucks the curls escaping my messy bun behind my ear and continues, "I needed to tell you that you mean so much to me too. What we had…it's 'more' to me too, and it always has been."

"I know," I say, my eyes clouded with tears.

"No, you don't," he shakes his head. "You don't know that I love you. I'm in love with you, Gem. I've known that I want you in my life, no, I need you in my life, since the moment I saw you flying off your bike," he releases a husky laugh.

I feel a surge of emotion running through my veins—emotions I've been experiencing for a while now, but struggled to put into words. The feeling I've been refusing to acknowledge and fighting to keep at bay is clear to me now. It's love.

"I love you too," I say, cry-laughing.

"You do?" he asks.

I don't know why he's surprised. Couldn't he tell that I'm completely and hopelessly in love with him from the way I look at him? From the way I always want to be near him? From the way I feel safe and at home around him? But I also understand that my leaving without saying goodbye must have communicated the opposite.

"Of course I do. No matter how hard I tried to fight it and no matter how hard I tried to deny it, I couldn't. I love you, Daan."

As soon as the words leave my mouth, he takes my lips in his, as if he's grateful for them for uttering those words. He kisses me with passion and emotion that only a person who is deeply in love can kiss. I cling to his neck and kiss him in a way that I hope will tell him how much I love him too.

He pulls away just a little, resting his forehead against mine. "I want to try this, G," he says. "I want to give us a chance to make this work. Fuck no strings attached; fuck distance. I want to do this with you."

I say nothing. I want to try this too. But I'm scared. I'm scared of all the ways this could fail. The reality is that even if we love each other, not much has changed. The reasons why we shouldn't be together still remain. I still have trust issues, and we still live thousands of miles apart. I'm not sure if just loving each other would be enough to make things work.

"I know you might need time to make a place for me in your life and to fully trust me. But I'll wait. You're worth the wait," he says, interrupting my train of thought. He then cups my face and lightly grazes my lips. My heart flutters in my chest with every touch and every word.

"I want to try too. But we both know it's hard to make a long-distance relationship work." My guards are coming down quickly, but I give my realistically skeptical side a last opportunity to make its case—to play the devil's advocate.

"I don't know about you, but when I want something...when I really want something, I'll work for it, I'll fight for it. And I want you more than anything, and I'm willing to work and fight for you. Are you willing to do the same for me? For us?" he asks, looking at me hopefully.

I've never had someone who wanted me so badly that they're willing to work to be with me, to fight for me. I feel a comforting warmth flood my body.

There might be a few reasons why Daan and I shouldn't be together. But just standing here with Daan, I realize there are a hundred more reasons why we should be together, why we should at least give 'us' a chance. The timing and the place might not be right, but Daan is the right guy, and that surpasses everything else. And who knows? Maybe distance will give us an opportunity to be intentional and to work for our love and connection every day. And Daan is worth putting in that work.

So I say, "I am… I'm willing to work and fight for you. For us."

I see the concern and worry wash away from his face, replaced by a warm, bright smile—a smile I've dearly missed. I'll do anything to make him smile like this, to make him happy. At this moment, I know he'll do the same for me too. He'll do anything to make me happy.

"I love you so much, G," he tells me again.

I don't know if I've ever felt as loved as I do at this moment. I might not know what the future holds for Daan and me. I might not know if we can make long distance work. I might not know if Daan would never leave me and break my heart. But this feeling of being seen, being loved, and being comfortable around another person is worth risking heartbreak. How I feel about Daan is stronger than my fears. So, I decide to embrace all the uncertainty and the unknown for the sake of us.

We spend every minute of the next two days together. It's the best weekend I've ever had. Being with Daan every day feels like the most natural thing. Having him in my space feels like he's always been here. Our lives mesh together as if this is the natural course they are always supposed to take.

When it's finally time to say goodbye, I don't feel the hollowness I felt when I left Amsterdam. I know we'll always stay connected and close to each other's hearts. So I feel hopeful and in love. Before he leaves, he holds me tightly for a long time and whispers in my ear, "Next time, meet me in Amsterdam."

Epilogue

One year later

I nervously pace back and forth in the arrival terminal of Schiphol Airport. Gemma is landing in Amsterdam in a few minutes for one of our regular visits, plus to celebrate our one-year anniversary. My nervousness has nothing to do with any of that though. Well, maybe a little. I'm excited and happy to see G, but I'm nervous about how she'll receive the news I'm going to share with her. News that changes a lot in both of our lives.

After a full year of a long-distance relationship, I'm finally moving to New York. I have been working on this plan for a few months—applying for jobs and looking for places to live. But I haven't told Gemma yet. I wanted to be certain about moving first and surprise her when the time comes. And now, the time has come. A month ago, I got a job offer in New York that is perfect for me.

I accepted the job offer and sold my apartment in Amsterdam, so there is no looking back as far as I'm concerned. I've also been looking for an apartment in New York that is big enough for both of us. Yes, I'm not just telling her I'm moving to her city to be closer to her, but I'm also asking her to move in with me.

I'm now doubting my decision to keep things from her until it's final. Maybe I should've discussed this with her and gotten her opinion on it before completely dismantling my life.

276

After all, this is a big change that affects both of us. When you're in a serious relationship, you're supposed to run major decisions by your significant other. I did the exact opposite of that.

So it's not surprising that I'm feeling extra nervous to see her and share the information. It's like the nervousness you feel when you're about to propose. What I'm planning to do is actually not too far from proposing. After all, I'm proposing to move across the Atlantic and disrupt her life and her routine.

G and I spent the last year traveling back and forth every chance we got. We spent our summer holiday together traveling within Europe; we celebrated Christmas and welcomed the New Year in New York. We talked on the phone every day and texted constantly throughout the day. I've never been more glued to my phone than I did this past year. We've fallen asleep FaceTiming or talking on the phone countless times. Despite the thousands of miles between us, we stayed close. As we promised, we worked hard to stay connected and close despite the distance. But it's time to be physically close. I will give anything to wake up next to Gem every day, to make her smile, and see her dimples dip.

I still remember the day I met her as if it were yesterday. When I left my house that morning for a run, the last thing I expected was to meet the love of my life. Someone falling off a bike in the center of Amsterdam? That I expected. After all, I live in a city where there are more bikes than people. So, when I saw a woman falling off her bike, I rushed to help her as I'd for anyone in that situation. I didn't help her because she was the most beautiful woman I'd ever met or because she looked lost and overwhelmed. I helped her simply because she was in need.

But when I helped her up and she looked at me, everything changed. It was as if my heart had stopped beating for a whole minute. I know that's not accurate physiologically speaking, but that's how overwhelming the feeling was.

I'm not saying it was love at first sight. I don't think I believe in that. Love requires choosing to be with someone for all they are—good or bad. Love is seeing someone at their worst, but still choosing to love them. That doesn't happen the first day you lay eyes on someone. It's built through however long it takes to know that you would do anything for that person and you would choose them no matter what. That only took two weeks for me.

So, what I felt when our eyes met for the first time was this inexplicable attraction, like I was supposed to be close to this person. Like I'd do anything to be around this person. Like I could just stare at her deep brown eyes for days and not get bored. The only problem was that I used to get so nervous around her that I averted my gaze whenever she looked at me. Well, that was the second problem. The first problem was she didn't want to be around me. She refused to give me her number.

But I'm a lucky bastard; she turned out to be my sister's friend and bridesmaid, whom I had been hearing about for years, but I hadn't had a chance to meet. When Sophie teamed us up to work on wedding tasks, I was rejoicing on the inside, although I had to protest a little to save face. I was ready to be her chauffeur and translator in a heartbeat.

I just wanted to be around Gemma. It didn't matter whether she wanted to be just my friend. It didn't matter whether she wanted to be friends with benefits, no strings attached. I was willing to be whatever or whoever she wanted me to be just to be around her.

I look up when I see a slew of travelers coming out of the arrival gate. Then I see her, and my heart jumps. Yes, my heart still does that, even though we've been together for a year. She starts running toward me when she sees me. She does this every time. She runs across the airport until I wrap her in a tight hug.

When we get home, I nervously hand her my job offer letter.

"What's this?" she says cautiously.

"Read it," I say, planting a kiss on her lips. When she's this close to me, I can't keep my hands off her. I can't help but touch her.

I see her read the letter, and I closely follow her expression. She looks confused at the beginning, and then I see her face slowly beam with a smile as the realization dawns on her.

She looks up at me, her beautiful smile coating her face. "You're moving to New York?"

"Yeah," I say sheepishly.

"Oh my God, babe," she exclaims and jumps up at me. I catch her by the waist and hold her close. This is the best reaction I could get for making this big of a decision without consulting her.

She looks at me in the eyes, her hands wrapped around my neck. "No more long distance?"

"No more long distance," I say.

"You have no idea how happy I am." She kisses me all over my face to show me how happy she is, as if saying it in words alone does not do it justice.

Then she looks at me as if she remembers something important. "But you don't like living in New York?" she says, a concern running across her expressive eyes.

"I like living wherever you are," I say, and I mean it. It doesn't matter that New York was not my first choice for living. But knowing that the love of my life lives there has changed how I feel about the city. It's the people that make a place. Deciding to move to New York was not a difficult decision at all.

But I can still see a concern lingering on her face. "Babe, I don't want you to be miserable and resent me."

It's impossible for me to be miserable when I get to live close to her and see her gorgeous face every day. Resenting her is unthinkable. Plus, she's never asked me to move to her city. I made that decision all by myself.

"You're my home, Gem. I'm happy wherever you are. I can handle gross subways and rats if I get to come home to you," I say, chuckling.

She laughs too, her beautiful smile washing away all the concern and worry from her face. God, I love this woman.

"Can we live together when I move to New York?" I ask, dropping the next major bomb.

"Of course, I'll be there every day to annoy you. Prepare to be sick of me," she laughs.

Getting sick of her would be unimaginable. After a year of living thousands of miles apart, working, and sometimes even fighting to stay connected, we get to live together. We get to go to bed and wake up next to each other every day. And I wouldn't have it any other way.

Other books by the author

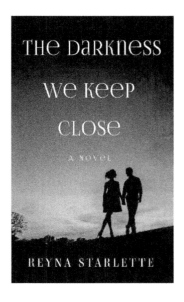

When Tanya and Reid first met, it was hardly a meet-cute. Tanya was an ambitious human rights lawyer who recently moved to DC to start her dream job. Reid was an FBI agent pursuing a serial killer terrorizing the DMV area. Their paths crossed when Tanya moved to Reid's apartment building. As their first tumultuous encounter turned into attraction and then love, their personal and professional lives intertwined in an unexpected way. In a way that threatened their very survival.

A story that combines a heartwarming romance and a gripping crime thriller.

Printed in Great Britain
by Amazon